The Lost Girl

Shifter Academy: United #2

Scarlett Haven

Cover by Kate Hall Book Covers
Edited by Ms. Correct All's Editing & Proofreading Services
Proofread by Zoe's Author Services

Thursday, September 8
No.

My heart stammers as I look into black eyes. Those eyes belong to somebody who is a good foot and a half taller than me and his biceps are literally the size of my waist. He smirks because he thinks he's got me. He may be bigger than me, but he's not faster.

I dart to the left, squeezing between him and the wall. His hand reaches out for me, but it barely grazes my skin as I run for it.

Heavy footsteps come up behind me. My own footsteps are silent, not making a noise as my feet hit the floor, but his are so loud, shaking the ground as he runs. If we were in the woods right now, all prey would be fleeing with all the ruckus he's making.

But while I am fast, I can't hold my speed for long. I just haven't been trained enough. So the heavy footsteps quickly catch up to me, and an arm goes around my waist, lifting me from the ground. I am tackled, I think. It's more like I'm being gently laid on the ground, because God forbid if I get a bruise during training.

His arm pins me in place. There is no way I can get out of this, just because he's a lot stronger than me. I go limp, accepting my defeat.

Mateo shakes his head back and forth. "You're not supposed to give up."

Yeah, I know. But it seems pointless to fight now. I've already lost, and we both know it.

I've been at Shifter Academy for three weeks now, and it's been two weeks since Mateo won the alpha challenge, earning me a spot in his pack. Since then, we haven't even had time to celebrate. Between Mateo needing time to heal from the silver knife, and our classes, we've hardly had time for *anything*. Not even training. But Mateo has decided it's time for me to learn how to fight now. And we've been going at this for about two hours. I'm not getting any better. In fact, I think I'm getting progressively worse as the session goes on.

As he pins me on the ground, he holds his weight off me enough so that he doesn't crush me, but he applies just enough to keep me down. I'm supposed to somehow get away. And I've tried getting away plenty of times tonight. But now, I think I'm ready to be caught.

I reach a hand up, tracing Mateo's cheek with my thumb gently. His black eyes fade back to their chocolate color and his face softens.

"Layla," he breathes out my name, reaching his own hand up to cup mine. "I guess we've worked hard enough tonight, but we have to keep doing this. No wonder your pride used you as a punching bag. You don't fight back."

"I don't want to fight you." I never want to fight any of my mates. And fighting my pride would've only made my beating worse. I just accepted them, and they were over quickly.

He smirks. "What am I going to do with you?"

"I have a few ideas." My voice comes out in a whisper, but I know that Mateo heard me from the way his body stiffens. Or maybe it's the smell lingering in the air that has made him pause.

My mates have been so patient with me, waiting until I am ready to complete the mate bond. I don't want to wait anymore, though. I want to make Mateo mine. I want them all to be mine.

Mateo pushes himself up off the floor, holding out a hand to help me up. "We should head back to our dorm and get ready for tonight."

Tonight, the pack is having a party to welcome me. Mateo winning the alpha challenge is definitely something that should be celebrated. I'm so glad to finally be away from my pride. The last few weeks may have been busy, but it's also the happiest I've ever been.

Happiness isn't something I thought was attainable for me. The women in my pride who taught me in school deliberately didn't tell me about things pertaining to the mate bond simply because they didn't think anybody would want me. I was taught that I was ugly—so ugly that no man would ever want me. And I never questioned it, not until I met the guys. Now, I realize I am pretty. My pride is just a bunch of narrow-minded idiots.

I accept Mateo's hand letting him pull me up from the ground. He does so effortlessly.

"Hey, Mateo." I push a piece of hair behind my ear, looking up at him. "Why do I get the feeling that you're pushing me away right now?"

He blinks. "I have no idea what you're talking about."

I take a deep breath, trying to pluck up the courage to speak. I want to be brave and honest with him right now, but I'm finding that sometimes it's harder than it sounds. I guess after being rejected by my pride for so long, I now fear being honest with my mates. I don't want them to reject me too. I think that's part of the reason we haven't completed our mate bond yet. Because I'm too scared to tell them I'm ready—I'm so ready.

"I want to make you mine," I admit, chewing on the corner of my bottom lip. "I don't want to wait anymore. I want to complete the mate bond."

He gazes at me with wide eyes saying nothing at all. And I stand there, holding my breath.

It's terrifying to be vulnerable like that.

Mateo shuts his eyes, taking a deep breath through his nose. When he reopens them, my heart sinks.

He frowns, shaking his head. "I'm sorry, Layla. We can't."

It's hard to breathe as the emotions wash over me. My bottom lip trembles and I can't help the negative thoughts that creep in.

Mateo doesn't love me. He doesn't want to bind his soul to mine. He's not attracted to me. Maybe… maybe the members of my old pride were right. Maybe I *do* need a paper bag over my head for somebody to want to mate with me.

I turn away from him as a tear rolls down my cheek. I don't want him to see me crying. Because even though he hurt me, I don't want to do the same to him. If he knows how devastated I am, he will feel guilty. He shouldn't feel bad for not wanting to mate with me.

"Layla." His voice breaks as he pulls me into his arms.

I want to fight him, but he's already proved he's stronger than me. I let him pull me into his arms, but I tense up at his embrace. The truth is, I don't want Mateo to comfort me right now.

"You're breaking my heart." He tightens his arms around me, but I don't give in.

I'm breaking *his* heart? He's the one who rejected me, not the other way around.

"It isn't that I don't want to be with you. I do." He kisses the top of my head so gently, like he's scared he's going to break me. "But I can't be your first, Layla. Ask one of the others."

My chest tightens and I step back from his embrace. I open my mouth to speak, but nothing comes out.

Mateo reaches out a hand to touch me, so I take another step back, needing space.

His face falls. "I don't want to hurt you, Layla. I want you so much that it physically hurts. But my bear would be too close to the surface. I wouldn't be able to hold back. Your first time should be with somebody who can take his time and be gentle."

My shoulders relax and my chest finally stops aching. I take a step closer to him. "Mateo, I don't care if you hurt me. I just want to be close to you. I want to make you mine forever."

"You should care if I hurt you." He is the one who steps back now. "How can you even say that?"

I take another step forward, closer to him. I'm not going to let him pull away from me. "Because I don't care. And I trust you. I know you won't hurt me."

"You don't know that for sure." His entire face falls, and he looks down at the ground. He feels so strongly about this. How can I show him that he's wrong? I know that he won't hurt me.

"Yes, I do." I reach a hand up, touching his forearm. "Mateo, I'm choosing you. Right now. I want you to be my first—for us to be each other's first."

Mateo takes a step back again, and he swallows hard. "We should go and get ready for the party tonight."

My stomach tightens, but I try to smile. "Okay."

Even my own mate doesn't want me.

I guess I'll always be the unwanted runt.

Welcome to the pack!

I try to push all of my negative thoughts aside as I get ready for the party. Mateo's mom and dad are both going to be there tonight. While I have met Alpha Scott, I haven't spent that much time with him, and I haven't met Mateo's mother at all. I don't even know her name.

I rub my sweaty palms on the front of my skirt, taking a deep breath. My heart is racing and I'm having a little trouble breathing.

"You okay?" Levi puts his hand on my back, gently rubbing.

I nod, letting out a breath. "Yeah, just nervous about tonight."

He cocks his head. "Something else is bothering you. I can feel sadness coming from you."

I shrug, not wanting to get into *that*. Not right now.

My chest still aches from Mateo's rejection. No matter what his excuses are, he's still turned me down. Mateo doesn't want to complete our mate bond. Just thinking about it causes tears to fill my eyes, but I refuse to let them fall. Now isn't the time.

Zoey came over to help me do my hair and makeup. If I cry, all of her hard work would have been for nothing. I swallow hard. "Levi, I'm fine. I promise. Just really nervous about meeting Mateo's mom."

He narrows his eyes, but nods. "Tonight will be fun."

"Are you coming?" I sit down on the couch, waiting for Mateo to come get me. He's really the last person I want to hang out with tonight, but I don't exactly have a choice.

"Nah. I've got stuff going on with my pride tonight. Kai will be coming with me, but I think Tucker is going to be there with you." Levi takes a seat beside me, putting his hand on my thigh.

I'm glad that Tucker will be there. He can be a buffer for Mateo and me. Or maybe I can avoid Mateo all night, and hang out with only Tucker. That sounds great too.

The door to our room opens, and I look over to see Mateo enter. My heart sinks at the sight of him.

He looks handsome—he's wearing a nice pair of jeans, a button up shirt, and a dinner jacket. But seeing him is too much right now, so I cast my gaze down.

"You ready?" Mateo asks.

I nod, clearing my throat.

Levi squeezes my thigh. "Hey, are you sure you're all right?"

I don't know if I'm all right. "You said Tucker is going, right?"

"Yeah." Levi glances from me to Mateo, running his hand over the back of his neck.

"Maybe I can go with him instead." I return my gaze down as I say it, not wanting to look at Levi or Mateo right now. I wish I could hide.

Mateo huffs.

Levi puts his hand on my chin, gently urging me to look at him. "You're being welcomed into Mateo's pack tonight as his mate. It's fitting that you go with Mateo."

A single tear falls, so I quickly wipe it away. "Fine."

I stand from the couch, walking toward Mateo. I keep my head down.

"Layla." Mateo says my name so softly, like a whisper.

I want to look up at him. I almost do on reflex, but I can't. Does he not see how much he's hurt me? "I'm ready to go."

He sighs.

I glance over at Levi, waving at him. "See you after the party."

"Bye." Levi waves, but he looks at Mateo, his eyebrows drawn together. "Take care of our girl, okay?"

Mateo doesn't respond. He just puts a hand on my back, gently nudging me forward.

We walk through the hallway of the castle, and then down the stairs. Neither one of us uttering a word to each other the entire time, and I am okay with that. The truth is, I don't know what I could say to him right now. He hurt me, he knows he hurt me, and that's that.

Mateo pulls me to a stop just outside of the front doors. "Tonight is supposed to be a celebration. Just try to pretend like you don't hate me, okay?"

Pretend that I don't *hate* him? But I don't hate him. I'm falling in love with Mateo. I know that. "I don't hate you. You just hurt my feelings."

I expect him to say something to that, but he doesn't. Not one word. He just grabs my hand and pulls me out the front door. He helps me climb onto a golf cart that is parked out the front. I look out the side, away from him, as he is getting into the driver's seat.

Mateo pauses, turning to me. "Just… don't let me ruin your night, Layla. You're free from the panthers, and it is something that should be celebrated. I'm really happy to have you be part of my pack."

I nod, wiping another tear away. "Thank you for fighting Alpha George for me."

He sighs, starting the golf cart. He takes off, not saying another word to me.

I don't know how I'm supposed to react. Maybe I am being silly for being so upset, but I can't help how I feel. Mateo hurt my feelings. If this were any other day, I'd be hanging out with one of my other mates. But tonight is important. Mateo is introducing me to his pack, and they are welcoming me as one of their own. It's supposed to be a happy day, but it's not.

I wish I had never told Mateo that I wanted to mate with him. That's what caused this whole stupid problem in the first place.

I spot lights twinkling ahead. I smell the barbecue cooking, and I see the members of my new pack that have come out to support me.

Not all of the pack is here—just Mateo's family and the ones who are young enough to attend Shifter Academy. But this is incredible. They're doing all of this for *me*.

My old pride had celebrations, but they were all in honor of Alpha George. He would *never* have a party to celebrate somebody else's success.

Mateo pulls to a stop in front of the party, and all thoughts of being hurt by what Mateo said are pushed to the back of my mind. I'm not going to let what happened ruin the rest of my day. I want to enjoy this moment.

Mateo walks around the golf cart and grabs onto my hand. He smiles, but I can feel how stressed he is through our mate bond. I try to block his feelings because my own are enough to deal with right now. I can barely breathe, and tears press against the back of my eyes. I scan the crowd, forcing a smile, and I look for Tucker. The first chance that I get to run away to him, I am going to do it.

Tucker is standing by a guy who is cooking burgers on a grill. He has his hands stuffed in the front pocket of his jeans, and he's laughing at something the guy said. He looks up, his eyes meeting mine, and he smiles at me, revealing his dimples. My heart flutters at the sight of him.

Mateo pulls me. "Come on."

I follow him toward where his dad is standing. Zoey is standing there too, along with a woman I don't recognize. I'm assuming that she's Mateo and Zoey's mom. Zoey looks just like her, except instead of chocolate brown eyes, hers are blue.

"Layla, I'd like you to meet my mother, Mary Fisher." Mateo's grin is genuine now, as he introduces me to his mom. "Mom, this is my mate, Layla Rosewood."

I expect Mary to try and shake my hand, but she surprises me by pulling me in for a hug.

I am *not* used to hugs. Even though my mates hug me all the time, it's still a lot to get used to. So I am dumbfounded by the fact that she is hugging me. We haven't even *spoken* to one another yet. But even I can't deny how nice of a hug it is. She's warm, and she smells faintly of vanilla. It makes me wonder what it would be like to hug my own mother. And I suppose Mary kind of is my mother, or at least she will be once Mateo and I complete our mate bond.

Which apparently might never happen.

I push those thoughts away as we part.

"You're just lovely," she gushes, grabbing onto the end of my hair. "What a lovely shade. I hope my grandchildren get your hair color."

Mateo groans. "Mom! Stop! You're going to scare her away."

She waves him off, just grinning.

Zoey laughs. "Mateo, if your ugly face hasn't scared her away, I don't think anything will."

Mateo rolls his eyes at his sister.

My chest burns, and I rub at it. It takes a moment for me to realize that what I'm feeling is jealousy. I'm *jealous* of Mateo's family. I want what he has so bad. I want a mom and dad who love me. I even want a little sister to tease me.

"Welcome to the pack, Layla." Alpha Scott walks closer, standing in front of me. He crosses his arms over his chest. "Is everything going okay? Are any members from your old pride bothering you?"

I shake my head. "Everything is good. They don't even look my way."

They probably don't look because they're scared of Kai and Mateo. Now that Jack, Brady, and their whole gang is gone, they have stayed quiet. I'm not sure if that's good or if they are just plotting and biding their time.

I stand and talk with Mateo's family for a little while longer. Every once in a while, somebody will approach and welcome me to the pack. It feels good to belong, but as soon as I possibly can, I head toward Tucker. My chest aches so bad when I'm around Mateo, and I just need a break. I know that Tucker will make me feel better.

Along the way, I spot Brittany and Angela. The two of them glare at me as I walk past, and I realize that maybe not everybody in the pack is glad to have me. But most are.

For the first time, I don't care what everyone thinks. I'm not going to let Brittany and Angela ruin the warm welcome

I've received. It doesn't matter if they don't want me here, because I *am* here. I'm a member of this pack now, and I'm not going to let a couple of mean girls bring me down.

I'm stronger than I used to be.

Love confessions.

As soon as I approach Tucker, he pulls me into his arms, rubbing his hand on my back. "Hey, what's wrong?"

I love that he knows right away that something is wrong. All my mates do. They know me so completely.

I pull back so I can look at him. "It's nothing."

He raises an eyebrow, calling me on my bluff. "Wolves can smell lies, remember?"

I sigh, considering telling him that I don't want to talk about it, but maybe I should talk to Tucker about it. "You know how Mateo started to train me today?"

He nods.

"Well… after training, I told Mateo that I was ready." My cheeks grow warm. "Uh, you know. For… mating."

Tucker chuckles, kissing me on the forehead. "Hey, I'm your mate. You don't have to be embarrassed about these kinds of things, okay?"

I nod. I know that in theory, but I am still embarrassed about it. "Mateo didn't want to complete the mate bond. He told me no."

He opens his mouth, then closes it, cocking his head to the side. "Why the hell would Mateo tell you no?"

"He said it's because he would hurt me." I chew on the side of my lip. "But Tucker, he wouldn't do that. I *know* he wouldn't. I think he was just saying that to let me down easy, or maybe to try and spare my feelings."

He grabs onto my hand. "Come on. Let's go for a walk."

A walk sounds nice. As wonderful as this party has been, all I've wanted all night was to get away.

Guilt floods me. This whole party is for me. It's to celebrate me and welcome me to the pack. Shouldn't I feel more excited about it?

It has been wonderful. I love Mateo's family, they're great. And hanging out with Zoey was fun.

Once Tucker and I are a little ways from the party, he sits down on the sand, pulling me into his lap. I turn to face him and see that he is watching me.

"When I was in my old pride, I was told that I was so ugly that I would need to cover my face before anybody would want to mate with me. And even though, deep down, I know that Mateo doesn't think that, it makes me think maybe those guys were right. Maybe I am ugly." I lower my head, shaking. "I already know you're going to tell me I'm beautiful. All of you guys say it all the time, and I was starting to believe you. But when Mateo rejected me…"

Tucker tightens his grip around my waist. "Layla, you *are* beautiful, and I know Mateo feels the same way. It's just…" He pauses, as if searching for the right words. He takes a deep breath, letting it out slowly. "Mateo doesn't have a lot of control when it comes to you. He is just so crazy about you that he kind of loses himself. I think he's worried that he'll lose control of his bear when you guys mate and that he will hurt you."

"But that's dumb. I know Mateo would never hurt me." I trust him. So why can't he trust himself?

"You and I know that, but he doesn't. Just be patient with him." Tucker reaches up, pushing a piece of hair behind my ear. "You are incredibly beautiful. Never doubt that."

My face grows warm at his compliment. "I'm still mad at Mateo."

He grins. "I know."

I lean into his shoulder. "It was a lovely night. Nobody has ever celebrated *me* before. My old pride never really celebrated anything. Any time Alpha George called a pride meeting, it was usually to brag about something he did."

"You should always be celebrated, Layla." Tucker kisses my forehead.

I sigh. "I don't know if I really fit in with the bears."

He chuckles. "A panther among bears is definitely unique."

Unique for sure. And while all my new pack mates seemed very welcoming, I wonder how they will feel when they see how small my panther is.

Tucker nudges my chin. "What caused this frown?"

I shake my head. "Nothing."

I don't want to get into *that* again. Tucker doesn't like when I talk about myself negatively. It's something I'm trying to work on, but it's not something I can just change overnight.

"Do you understand that Mateo didn't turn you down because he thinks you're ugly?" Tucker asks.

I bite the corner of my lip and shrug. I guess I know in *theory*, but my heart and my head feel like they're saying two very different things.

Tucker shakes his head. "I am going to kill him."

"Please don't do that." Mateo doesn't deserve to die for turning me down. It's his decision. "I think I just need time to get over his rejection. It's hard, but I respect that he doesn't want me like that."

He growls. "Layla, you are completely oblivious sometimes. But I can't even be mad at you because it's not your fault. Your pride completely messed with your head. They made you believe all these horrible things, and I don't know how to fix it."

I gasp as I look at him. I had no idea that Tucker felt that way. "What my old pride did doesn't matter. What matters is this. What matters is *us*, Tucker."

He gently caresses my cheek with his thumb. "You're right. Your old pride doesn't matter anymore. You're free of them. I just hope that you are able to see past the things they told you. They abused you for years, and that isn't going to go away overnight."

I know he is right. My old pride *did* abuse me. I just try not to think of it in that way.

"They made you feel like you're not attractive, and I hate that." His cheeks are red, and his knuckles are white from the fist he makes.

I grin at his protectiveness, tracing a finger along his knuckle. "But you make me feel beautiful. And that has to count for something, right?"

His lip turns up on one corner and he shakes his head slightly. "How do you always know what to say?"

"I don't. You do. You make me feel pretty, which is something I never thought I would feel. I believed the lies. Every summer, my hair would get lighter in the sunlight, and my skin would turn golden. My pride, they would stay pale. And their hair would always stay the same black color. And I thought there was something wrong with me." I shake my head. "I tried staying out of the sunlight to see if it would help, but it only made my hair turn red, which was worse."

He smiles, but it quickly fades. "I wish I would've known about you. If I had, I could've rescued you from them."

My heart swells as I look into his light brown eyes. "Tucker, we were kids. You couldn't have done anything. The timing was perfect."

"But the abuse..."

I cut him off. "The abuse doesn't matter."

He nods, but his body is still tense.

"Just knowing that you care is enough. I never thought anybody would ever care about me." I gently rub my fingers down his arms. "You know, the panthers aren't really religious, but I used to pray that somebody would find me and rescue me. When I was little, I hoped it would be my mom. But as I got older, I started to hope for a mate. Even though I knew I wasn't pretty enough, I just hoped that I'd find a mate that thought I was pretty. And it took a little while, but you're here now. And all the abuse was worth it, because I have you, Tucker."

He licks his lips, his eyes trained on me. "I love you, Layla."

I gasp. "What?"

Certainly he didn't say what I thought he just did.

"I love you," he repeats.

Love?

Tucker loves me.

I've never been loved in my entire life. Not by anybody. And yet, this beautiful wolf just declared his love for me, and I don't know how to react. My heart is racing, and my stomach feels like it's full of butterflies.

"I love you too," I breathe out, because it's true.

I've been in love with him for a little while now, I've just been too scared to admit it to myself. I was afraid that if I allowed myself to fall for him that he wouldn't feel the same way. But he *does*.

We're in love.

He smiles so big, his eyes lighting up. "I didn't know if you would say it back."

"How could I not?" I shake my head in disbelief. How could Tucker *ever* feel insecure. He's so perfect.

He smirks. "I am excited for when we complete our mate bond. Not just because of the physical pleasures, though I am excited about that. But I want you to see yourself through my eyes. I want you to see just how much I love you. I want you to feel it."

My breath catches in my throat.

Tucker *wants* to be with me in that way.

I know that tonight isn't the right time to complete our mate bond. There are people not that far down the beach who could hear and see us if they wanted. And the same day I get rejected by Mateo isn't the right time. But the fact that Tucker wants to, is enough for now.

"You already make me feel loved." I peek at him through my lashes, my heart racing. "I feel desirable."

He grins. "Good. Because you *are* desirable."

I close my eyes, letting the words sink in.

Tonight started off so horribly, but it is going to end on a much happier note.

I shift on his lap, and I feel something poke me in the butt. It takes a second to realize *what* poked me. My face burns. "Sorry."

His own face turns pink. "I told you that you're desirable."

My face is still burning with embarrassment, but my stomach flutters. My breath catches in my throat. "Tucker?"

"Yeah?"

I cast my gaze down, not wanting to see his face while I say what I need to. "I know that it's different for girls than it is for guys, but I... I am... turned on... too." I stutter over my words, my face growing warmer.

"I know. I'm a shifter, Layla. I can smell your desire."

Right. I knew that.

I clear my throat.

"But it makes me feel good to know that you feel the same as me." He squeezes my hand.

I lie back against Tucker's chest, watching as the waves gently crash onto the shore.

I am loved.

And I am *in* love.

Nothing in the world has ever been more perfect than this moment.

Friday, September 9

The impasse.

When I walk out of the bathroom on Friday morning ready to head to breakfast, I find that everybody, aside from Mateo, has left. Which definitely means that Mateo is going to want to talk to me. And as much as I *know* we need to talk, I kind of don't want to.

I walk toward the door, hoping that I can just get him to follow me to the dining hall, but I should know better. Mateo gently grabs onto my arm as I pass him, pulling me to a stop.

My skin tingles where he touches me. And through his touch, I can't deny the connection that we have.

I take a deep breath and turn to face him. But I don't look up to meet his gaze. Instead, I focus on his chest. "Mateo, we should get to breakfast."

"We need to talk." He utters the words I've been dreading. But I know he's right. We do need to talk.

I sigh. "Okay. So talk."

He growls. "Layla..."

I want to forgive him. I want to just say 'I'm sorry.' I want to be able to tell him that I understand. But I *don't*. I'm not sorry, and I'm not ready to forgive him yet. I want to be mad at him a little bit longer. Not because I want to hold a grudge, but because I am still hurt.

It hurts to even take a breath when I think about what happened yesterday. Even now, it still brings tears to my eyes.

"I'm sorry," Mateo says.

"You hurt me." A tear falls from my eye. Even though I try hard to stop the tears, I can't.

"I know I did. And I am sorry."

"You already said that." I wipe the tears away with the back of my hand.

"Can you understand my point of view on this?" Mateo's voice is tight. "I don't want you to be hurt, emotionally or physically. But I can't guarantee I won't hurt you if we complete our mate bond. I don't want to be first. You should be with one of the other guys first."

I take a step back from him, needing a little space just to breathe. "You said that yesterday already."

"My answer hasn't changed since yesterday." He reaches out a hand to touch me, so I take another step back.

I cross my arms over my chest. "Then we shouldn't talk, because I also haven't changed my mind since yesterday."

"Tucker said he talked to you." Mateo's voice softens.

I nod. "He did."

"He said he explained my reasons."

I nod again.

"But you still can't understand?" His entire face falls as he looks at me.

"Did he tell you why I'm so upset?" I hug my arms tighter against myself.

He sighs. "Something about your old pride. They fucked you up."

"They told me I was too ugly to mate with—that for somebody to want me, I would have to wear a paper bag over my head for it to even be tolerable. They said any man would be disgusted to have to touch me." I wipe away the tears from my face forcefully. "I never thought I would even have a mate. Because certainly fate wouldn't be cruel enough to have somebody be fated to somebody as ugly as me."

"Layla—"

I cut him off. "And then I met Tucker. And you. And Levi and Kai. For the first time in my life, I felt pretty. And then you rejected me yesterday. I felt all those horrible feelings come back. I thought you didn't want me because my pride was right. I am ugly."

"That's not true." He raises his voice, taking a couple steps toward me. He puts a hand gently on the side of my cheek. "You're beautiful. So beautiful that sometimes it hurts to even look at you. I want you in that way. But I can't hurt you, Layla. If I was first, I might hurt you. I can't control my bear around you. He wants to claim you so bad. He has been yelling at me to make you mine since the very first day I laid eyes on you."

I open my arms. "Then do it, Mateo. I don't want to wait anymore."

He staggers backward, shaking his head. "I *can't*. If I did, I wouldn't be any better than the members of your old pride."

I take a step toward him. "You won't. I know you won't."

I see it the moment he makes up his mind. His face grows hard, and his shoulders stiff. "No. I'm not going to hurt you, and that is that."

My heart races and my body grows warm as I glare at Mateo. "You think I'm too weak to mate with you. You think that mating with you is going to break me."

"I didn't say that," he growls. "Stop putting words in my mouth."

"You think you're going to hurt me," I say.

He nods. "Yes."

"Because I'm a runt."

He growls again, his eyes turning black. "That's not what I said."

"But it's how you make me feel every time you reject me. You keep telling me you're scared of breaking me, and it makes me *feel* breakable."

But his face remains hard, and I *know* I'm not going to change his mind.

I let out a breath. "I don't think either one of us is going to change the other's mind. This argument is pointless."

He frowns. "But I don't want you to be mad at me."

"And I don't want you to think I'm breakable." I shrug. "But I don't think either one of us is going to get what we want. And I'm tired of arguing."

He rubs his hands over his face, groaning. "You are killing me."

"Same." I walk forward, heading toward the door.

Since we can't come to an agreement, I'm going to end this argument.

"Don't leave."

I grin at him over my shoulder as I open the door. I walk out, slamming it shut behind me. I hear him curse as he runs after me.

If I want Mateo to stop treating me like I'm broken, I am going to have to show him that I'm not as fragile as he seems to think I am.

Being a bad girl.

I've been mad at Mateo all day. The guys are amused, but Mateo seems to be getting frustrated. I would be frustrated if I were him too, but I just *need* to be mad at him right now. It makes me feel better to be angry with him.

After trig, Kai walks me toward my physical education class, but I really don't want to go.

This is my one class with Mateo. There will be no buffer between us, and there will be no getting away from him.

I stop in the middle of the hallway just outside of the door, putting my hand on Kai's arm. "Hey, can we ditch our last class?"

Kai smirks. "Layla, you really should stop avoiding Mateo."

"Probably. But not right now." I poke out my bottom lip. "Please? Can't we just go back to the room and hang out or something?"

"On one condition."

"What condition?" I ask warily.

"You have to talk to Mateo tonight." He raises an eyebrow, looking at me with his purple eyes.

"But... we talked this morning. And it didn't go well." I don't want to talk to Mateo.

"Then go to class." Kai turns to walk away.

"Or I could ditch without you." I hold my head higher.

He groans. "You're so stubborn."

I shrug. "What's it going to be?"

"I'll ditch with you, but you're not getting out of talking to Mateo." He grabs my hand, pulling me from the door as the final bell rings.

Mateo is probably going to be pissed when he realizes that I am *not* coming to class, but he will get over it.

Kai holds my hand as we walk toward our room.

I guess it's technically still *my* room until I complete the mate bond with them, but they've never left me alone in there. All four guys sleep in the room with me, rotating who gets to sleep with me on the bed. But that is something they *won't* compromise on. They force me to sleep on the bed, saying the cot is too uncomfortable for me.

Kai opens the door and we walk in. I sit down on the bed scooting up to the headboard and pull my knees up to my chest.

"I can't believe I let you talk me into ditching class," Kai muses as he sits down beside me. "You're a bad girl."

I roll my eyes, but grin. "This is way more fun than class."

Normally, training is my favorite class of the day. I get to hang out with Mateo while he trains me. And I get to hang out with Zoey, which is always fun. But since yesterday, Mateo is pretty much the last person I want to hang out with.

"You know you're driving Mateo insane, right?" Kai turns toward me. "He is crazy about you, and you being mad at him is eating him up."

I shrug. "He hurt me. You guys always get mad at me for not standing up for myself. So now I am standing up for myself."

He sighs. "We want you to get mad at your old pride. Not us."

I laugh, shaking my head. "Kai, that's not how it works."

He grins, cocking his head. "Yeah, maybe you're right."

"I don't want to talk about Mateo." I scoot closer to Kai, putting my head on his shoulder.

"Okay." He wraps his arms around me, kissing the top of my head. "You are so good at getting what you want."

"Apparently not that good, or else you wouldn't force me to talk with Mateo again tonight," I grumble.

He gives me a pointed look. "Layla, I know you want to talk to him. You don't like being mad at him any more than he likes you being mad at him."

I want to object, but we both know he's right. And he knows because of his fae powers. He can feel my emotions.

"Do you have to use your fae powers on me?" I lift my head, looking at him.

"I can't turn them off." He smiles sadly. "Sorry."

"It's not your fault." I sigh. "You're right. I don't really like being mad at Mateo. But being mad at him helps me feel better. He hurt me so bad, Kai. And maybe I'm stupid for feeling that way."

"It's not stupid. You can't help how you feel." He grabs my hand, gently caressing it with his thumb. "To be honest, I'm a little mad at him too. I don't get him. I don't get why he is telling you no. I *know* he wants you like that."

I chew on my bottom lip. "Really?"

He nods.

His words fill me with hope.

If *anybody* knows, it's Kai.

"Are you sure?" I ask.

"Yes."

Maybe... maybe Mateo truly is worried about hurting me.

I just wish he would trust himself.

"Did you have fun hanging out with Levi's pride last night?" I don't want to talk about Mateo anymore. I feel like all I ever do is talk to my mates about him, and I'm just over it.

He grins. "Surprisingly, yeah. I got to meet his alpha. Well... sort of alpha. She's his alpha in training. She's a true alpha, which I'm not exactly sure what that means, but she has three mates. And I talked to her about having multiple mates."

My eyes widen. "That must've been awesome. I'd love to talk to somebody with multiple mates."

"She says I should be nice to you, because all her mates always gang up on her." Kai laughs. "I guess we kind of do that to you too."

I nod. "Especially with the whole Mateo thing."

"Point taken."

I wonder what she was like.

I remember my pride talking about the true alpha for a little bit. I think Alpha George wanted her to join our pride, but she wasn't interested. I can't blame her. The tiger pride seems like it's a lot nicer.

I look over at Kai and find him watching me. His eyes are a light shade of pink as he studies me.

One time, I asked Kai what pink meant. He explained that it could mean lust or love. At the time, I didn't think Kai could love me yet. But now... now I wonder.

Last night, Tucker told me that he loves me. And since then, I have come to realize that I love *all* of my mates. Even

Mateo. Even though I am so furious at him, I am still head over heels for him.

Kai's eyes widen, and I wonder if he *felt* my feelings.

Still, feeling it and me telling him are different. And I want to tell him.

"Hey, Kai?"

"Hmm?" His pink eyes scan over my face, as if he's trying to memorize it.

"I love you."

He grins. "I know."

Of course he does.

"Layla Rosewood, you are my life. I love you with all of my heart and my soul." His pink eyes never leave mine.

Overwhelmed by my feelings, I lean forward and press my lips against Kai's.

I don't know what has gotten into me. I usually let the guys make the first move. I *never* kiss them first. But something about the way Kai was looking at me made me want to make the first move. I want to be brave. Especially with my mates.

I don't know why I've been so nervous to make the first move, because Kai doesn't reject me. He kisses me back.

With his kiss, he is showing me just how much he loves me, and I try to convey the exact same thing to him.

Kai lifts me easily, setting me in his lap. I straddle him, running my fingers through his hair. I wish our mate bond was complete so I could know what he was thinking right now.

I pull back a little to ask him, but when he opens his eyes, I see hot pink.

"Hot pink?" I question.

He breathes heavily. "It's a mix of lust and love."

I stare into his eyes for a moment longer, memorizing the shade. I want to remember this forever.

I lean forward to kiss him again, tangling my fingers in his hair. Kai grips onto my thighs, stroking them in a way that makes my head spin. My entire body feels like it's on fire, and my body is throbbing.

Kai pulls back a little bit. "I can feel your lust."

I slowly open my eyes, grinning at him. "Yeah?"

"Yeah." He smiles back. "And I want very much to take this further. But the guys are going to be walking through the door in about five minutes. And unless you want them to catch us in a very precarious position, we should probably stop."

"I don't want to stop."

He laughs. "We don't have to. I don't mind if we have an audience."

My eyes widen and I pull back. "No. You're right. Our first time should be for just us."

As my lust begins to subside, I know I've made the right decision. The thought of anybody *watching* me mate with Kai is embarrassing.

Maybe later.

But not for my first time.

Kai grins, leaning forward to kiss me again. This time, he keeps his hands gently on my back, and his kisses are soft and sweet. Still, I can feel how hard he is. I push those thoughts aside and just kiss him back, wanting to enjoy this perfect moment for a little bit longer.

Kai loves me. And I love him.

Nothing could ever be more perfect than it is right now.

Angry kissing.

Mateo is grumpy.

Really grumpy.

The other guys aren't making it any better either, because they keep teasing and taunting him.

His face turns red, and his eyes even go black.

I know that I've hurt him by acting the way I have, and that's *not* what I wanted.

Mateo stands abruptly, growling at Levi, cutting off his joke. "That's it. Everybody out."

The guys chuckle, getting up from their seats, heading toward the door.

I get up, feeling confused as to *why* he's kicking everybody from the room.

Mateo grabs my arm. "Not you, sweetheart. Just them."

I swallow hard, turning to watch the guys leave. Kai gives me a smile and a thumbs up as he walks out.

I flinch when the door latches shut. It takes me a few seconds to get up the nerve to turn to Mateo and look at him. "Why did you force them to leave?"

But then I see that his eyes are black.

Blacker than I've ever seen them.

His bear is so close to the surface. "I can't take you being mad at me anymore."

"And I can't handle you rejecting me anymore." I shouldn't taunt him when he's like this, but apparently I am feeling very brave, because I take a step closer to him. "You hurt me, Mateo. You hurt me more than I thought was possible to be hurt."

His black eyes fade to chocolate brown. "Layla."

Tears press against the back of my eyes. "The worst part is you *knew* just how bad you hurt me. You could feel it through the bond."

He looks at me, not saying a word.

"I'm so mad at you."

"I know." His voice is rough. "To be honest, I'm a little mad at you too."

Which is obvious.

"How do I fix this?" He covers his face with his hands for a second, then looks at me. "I don't know what to do."

I don't want to be mad at Mateo anymore. But it's not something I can just stop.

I shrug my shoulders. "I don't know. I think it's just something that takes time."

His eyes flash black again, but only for a second. "No. I refuse that answer."

"Well, that's the only answer you're getting. You can't just alpha your way out of this one, Mateo." I stand straighter, facing him head on. I am not going to let him intimidate me. Not today.

He takes a step forward, but I don't cower. Not even when his chest presses against mine. Well, more like his stomach against my chest. I have to crane my neck to look up at him, but I don't back up. I just stand there, crossing my arms over my chest.

Mateo picks me up and takes long strides over to the couch, where he promptly sits and settles me on his lap.

I wiggle, trying to get out of his grip.

"If we're going to have this conversation, it should be face to face. This is the only way I can look you right in the eyes." He smirks.

I groan. "You're so infuriating."

"I know."

I stop wiggling, turning to face him. "Why can't you just let me be mad at you?"

"Because I can't stand it." His voice breaks. "Yes, I knew that I hurt you. And I knew that I hurt you *badly*, but can't you feel how much you're hurting me now?"

I can. I feel a horrible pain in my chest, and I know that it's coming from Mateo. But I also have my own pain.

"Mateo," I breathe his name out.

"No. You can't do that." He shakes his head back and forth. "You don't get to play the victim right now."

Play the victim?

His words cause my blood to boil. "You're such a jerk."

"Maybe."

Maybe?

More like *absolutely*.

I want to punch somebody. Me, Layla, the most mild mannered person from the pride. Well, my old pride that is.

I grab onto Mateo's shirt, gripping it tightly. My fists turn white from gripping it so tightly. "You make me *so* mad."

"Yeah, well, same."

We aren't going to come to an agreement tonight, and arguing is just making things worse. So instead of using words, I tug on Mateo's shirt, pulling him closer. I press my lips against his—hard—and I kiss him. I show him just how angry I am at him through our kiss.

If we were human, I'm pretty sure my lips would bruise under the pressure. But we're not, and this kiss is exactly what I needed. And judging from the way his lips meet mine with just as much passion and angst, I'd say he feels the exact same way as I do.

I pour every single emotion that I've felt the past two days into the kiss. All of the anger, the hurt, the disappointment. I want it all gone. I'm tired of feeling this way, especially about my mate.

I untangle my fists from his shirt, and I put them in his hair. I gently pull on the ends, which causes Mateo to moan against my lips. I would *definitely* say that he likes that. And hearing him moan causes my heart to race even faster.

Am I turned on?

I never thought that angry kissing the hell out of somebody would turn me on, but then again this is my first time ever doing it. But getting turned on just reminds me that Mateo doesn't want me, which pisses me off again. It's a vicious cycle.

Mateo thinks he can break me.

Does he not realize that I'm already broken? I've been broken so many times that it hardly even hurts anymore. My body is numb to pain.

I grind my hips onto him, and I feel how hard he is as I rub myself against the front of his jeans.

So he is attracted to me. At least his body is.

He pulls back. "Layla, you have to stop."

But I don't want to stop. "Mateo, please."

"I don't want to hurt you." His chocolate brown eyes plead with me.

"We don't have to have sex. We can do other stuff. Could you handle that?" Tucker has pleased me with just his hand, and I very much liked that. I'd like to get the chance to do that for my mates.

"Just... let me touch you." Mateo's voice softens as he looks at me. "That's it, though. Just me touching you. Can you handle that?"

I nod.

Anything.

I just need something, but I don't know what.

Mateo kisses me again, this time softer, and I feel his hand on my thigh. He slowly moves it up, as if giving me a chance to move away if I want.

Yeah, that's not happening. I will stay right here, for a long as it takes, because I like very much where this is going.

But he moves his hand so slowly. I want to grab his wrist and guide his hand right to where I want it, but I promised him that I would let him do the touching. If I urge him to move faster, he might pull away altogether. And if he pulled away, I feel as though I would spontaneously combust.

I whimper as his fingers slowly graze against the side of my panties. He pushes them out of the way.

Mateo's fingers touch me, finally. He gently rubs his fingers against me, like he's trying to learn what I like. And maybe he is. Mateo confessed to me that he's a virgin. But after only a moment, he moves his fingers inside of me, touching just the right spot. It's like he knows my body thoroughly, even though he's just started touching it.

I squirm against him as he moves his finger in and out of me.

"Is that okay?" he whispers against my lips.

"Yes," I moan against his. "Please don't stop."

He chuckles, moving his lips down my neck, kissing me so softly while his fingers touch me in the most intimate ways. I am so close when he moves his thumb over my clit and begins to circle it while his fingers thrust inside of me. I moan as I find my release, pushing my head against his shoulder.

My entire body throbs in the best way as he moves his hand away.

"Was that okay?"

I look up, my eyes wide. "Are you kidding? That was incredible."

He grins. "Yeah? It was good for me too."

"But you're still..." I motion to the very hard body part in his pants.

"This is about you." He kisses my forehead. "That was the most beautiful thing I've ever seen in my life. You coming is... wow."

I chew on the corner of my lip. "Really?"

He nods. "How can you not see how crazy I am about you? Layla, you are my everything."

I suck in a breath. "Mateo, I'm sorry that I was so mad at you."

"I'm sorry that I hurt you."

Maybe there is no solution to our argument, at least not right now. Just because I'm ready to complete my mate bond with Mateo doesn't mean that he's ready. I have to respect that. I shouldn't have pushed him anyway.

"Will you forgive me? I know now that you're not ready. And I don't ever want to force you to do anything you don't want to." I look at him, hoping that I haven't screwed everything up.

"You think I don't want you in that way?" He furrows his brows, tilting his head. "Layla, I want you in every way that I can possibly have you. I want to make you mine forever. I want you so bad that it hurts. I just don't want to hurt you."

I sigh, touching the sides of his cheeks gently. "You are infuriating, and confusing. But you're mine. When you're ready, I'll be waiting."

Forever, if I have to.

Monday, September 12

Going too far.

On Monday, I don't ditch my physical education class. In fact, I'm excited about it. I'm glad that Mateo and I were able to work through our issues. It's not *resolved*, but it's definitely better than it was.

After class is over, Zoey and I head to the girls' shower room together. She has stuck by my side since I joined her pack. She's become a really good friend, much to Mateo's dismay. Though, I know he's just joking. He's glad I'm friends with his sister. He wants me to like his family.

Just as we are about to walk into the locker room, the teacher calls her over.

She offers me a smile and waves before walking off to leave me.

I don't have anything to worry about. I know that. Since I joined the pack, everybody has been nice. Well, other than Brittany and Angela. But aside from their glares, they haven't approached me again since that day Mateo told them to leave me alone.

Still, I find myself rushing through my shower, trying to get out of here quickly. But the locker room clears out rapidly today. Nobody heads to the showers, which I find odd. At least, until I spot Brittany and Angela walk in. They're fully clothed, and something tells me they're not coming in here to shower.

"Where's your bodyguard?" Angela saunters forward, a smile on her face. That girl hardly ever smiles, especially at me. "I didn't think you went anywhere without the bitch."

I have a really bad feeling about this.

"Zoey isn't my bodyguard. She's my friend." I won't let them talk bad about Zoey. "Don't call her a bitch. She's your alpha's daughter. She outranks you. You should be kind to her, respect her."

Respect is important. Even my old alpha, as flawed as he was, taught me that. If you can't respect your alpha then you really don't belong in the pride. And the only other option is being alone, which is a fate far worse than being in a pride that doesn't want you.

When you're a shifter and you don't have a pride or pack, you are truly alone. While the humans grow old around you, it's like you're frozen in time. You can't make friends or connections. It's truly the worst kind of torture a shifter could go through.

Brittany steps forward. "Should I respect you too? Because you're my future alpha's sex toy?"

I shiver, not meaning to. But I hear the malice in her tone. Brittany truly loathes me.

"Just get out of here." I turn off the water and am about to grab a towel. I know that most shifters are used to immodesty, but I don't like being unclothed in front of others. Not even females. But as I go to grab for the towel, Angela grabs onto my wrist with force, twisting my arm around.

I let out a whimper at the pain, but I remain quiet as Brittany comes up in front of me. Angela has my arm twisted behind my back. I try to fight against her, but she's a lot stronger than me. It's not a surprise, because I'm not strong. I just started training with Mateo, and I haven't learned a lot yet.

"How did you do it?" Brittany stops directly in front of me, looking down at me with a glare.

"Do what?" I pull my arm, trying to get free, but Angela won't budge.

"You know what." Brittany raises a hand, slapping me across the face. "Don't play innocent, you slut."

I place my free hand against my cheek where she slapped me. My face is stinging from the hit. There are tears in my eyes, but I don't let them fall. I won't give Brittany the satisfaction.

"How did you trick Mateo and those others into thinking they're your mates?" Her voice is hard. "Did you get a witch to cast a spell?"

"No. What are you talking about?" My voice rises a pitch. "Are you insane? You can't fake a mate bond."

She smacks me across the cheek again, this time on the other side. "You really are a slut. You not only stole my alpha, but you had to be greedy and steal three others."

I know that no matter what I say, she's going to keep hitting me. I decide to keep my mouth shut. It's not worth fighting her. Not when she's like this.

Brittany's mouth turns upward on one side. "This is how you're going to play it then?"

She swings her hand at me again, but this time her hand is balled up. Her fist hits me right in the eye with enough force that everything goes black for a second. I stumble forward, and Angela lets go of my wrist. Just as I'm about to gain my balance, I feel hands on my back, shoving me. I fall onto the ground, on my knees.

Brittany laughs. "On your knees like a good little slut."

"I'm not a slut." I know it's better to keep my mouth shut. It's two against one, and I can't win. I couldn't win if it was one against one. I'm simply not strong enough. But something in me can't let them keep talking to me like this. Maybe it's because I stayed quiet in my old pride. I let them say awful things about me as they beat me. But now I have a fresh start, and I don't want to be treated like that anymore. I don't want people to treat me like a runt.

Brittany kicks me in the side. She's wearing a pair of boots, and it hurts bad. I call out without meaning to. I don't want to give them the satisfaction of knowing how bad they're hurting me, but I'm pretty sure she broke a rib.

In that moment, I wonder if I should keep count. Should I start over counting how many bones my new pack is going to break?

One.

Another kick comes at me, this time from Angela. She has on a pair of tennis shoes, so it doesn't hurt quite as bad, but I know it'll leave a bruise.

Kick after kick is delivered, so I get on the ground, rolling myself up into a ball. I cover my head with my hands, and I make myself as small as possible. I know from way too much experience that I don't get hurt as bad if I do this. I try to think of happy things.

But thinking of happy things isn't easy when blow after blow keeps hitting me. Kick after kick hits my back and my sides. I know that I'm screaming, and I know that they will only get more enjoyment from my screams, but I can't help it.

I thought things would be different in my new pack. I thought there *had* to be kindness in the world. But maybe I was wrong. Maybe all packs are just as evil as my old pride is.

"Brittany, we got to go," a frantic voice says. I think it belongs to Angela, but I can't look up to see.

One more kick comes, right to my head. Everything gets hazy as I hear footsteps running away.

They're gone. Angela and Brittany aren't here to hurt me any longer. But I can't relax or let my guard down.

My old pride used to pretend like they were done. They would even pretend to walk away. And as soon as I relaxed, they start in again. I know better than to believe that it's over.

I hear another set of heavy footsteps. I tense up, thinking they're coming back.

"Layla."

It's not until I hear Mateo's voice that I finally relax.

I'm going to be okay. Mateo is here to save me.

I open my eyes, looking up at him. Everything is a little hazy, but I see him looking down at me.

"Mateo," I breathe out. "I knew you'd come."

I close my eyes, letting the darkness consume me.

Mateo is here.

Everything is good now.

I've had worse.

When I open my eyes again, all of my mates are there. I couldn't have been out long, because I'm still in the bathroom. I'm no longer on the floor. Mateo has me lifted into his arms and he holds me ever so gently.

I reach a hand out to touch his cheek, noticing the tears that are falling from his eyes.

"Don't cry," I whisper.

"Layla."

All of my mates crowd closer around.

"We should get her to the doctor," Kai suggests.

I shake my head. "I'm fine."

"Sweetie, you're not fine." Levi reaches a hand out, gently touching my cheek.

"I've had worse." Worse that I never went to the doctor for.

I think that must've been the wrong thing to say because my mates tense up. I even hear Tucker curse.Some

"Let's get her dressed first." Kai steps closer. "Are you okay with us dressing you?"

My cheeks grow warm as I realize that I'm definitely *not* wearing clothes. I was in the shower when Brittany and Angela decided to attack me.

Shifters don't care about modesty. But it's the first time my mates have seen me without clothes on. But none of them are looking at me in a sexual way—probably because I am covered in bruises. I can feel them all over my body, my back, my side, my face, my legs. It even hurts to breathe. I keep that to myself, not wanting to alarm my mates.

"I trust you." My voice is quiet as the words come out, but the words are true. My mates are the only people I really trust.

My mates carefully help me get dressed. They gather my clothes from my locker. I'm thankful that I packed a dress to wear after class today, because putting it on is easier. But them helping me put on my bra and underwear is a little awkward. But they are complete gentleman. They never once let their eyes linger, even though I wouldn't mind. I am theirs.

Once I am dressed, I try to walk forward. I limp a little because of the pain in my leg. I don't think it's broken, but it's bruised pretty good.

Tucker doesn't let me walk. He swoops me into his arms, and I don't protest. I rather like him carrying me. I put my arms around his neck, making it easier for him to carry me.

"Thank you," I whisper to him, laying my head on his chest. He's warm and comfortable. If my body didn't hurt so bad, I could fall asleep right now. "I think I have a concussion."

Tucker's body tenses at my words.

"Who did this to you?" Mateo asks. Well, he *demands* it as he growls at me.

I shake my head, not wanting to get Brittany and Angela in trouble. I know that they should be reprimanded for their actions, but not when Mateo is this angry. I don't want them to be killed. It isn't their fault that they don't like me. They think I stole their alpha from them.

Maybe I should hate them for what they did to me, but I don't. If anything, I feel sorry for them. To hate somebody so much that you kick them and beat them like that... they must have so much rage in their heart.

"You know you can't keep it a secret forever." Even Kai's voice sounds rough. He too is angry.

Of course he is. All of my mates are.

"I will tell you when you're not so angry," I promise them.

"Was it somebody within the pack?" Mateo asks.

I nod, allowing him the answer to that question.

"I'm going to fucking kill them." I don't have to see him to know that his eyes are black. His voice is basically a growl because his bear is so close to the surface.

I look beside us. Mateo is standing there, so I reach a hand out and touch his bicep. "Mateo, don't punish violence with violence. It's not right."

He sighs, glancing at me. His face softens and his shoulders relax. "You are far too nice of a person. Layla, you were just beaten up, and you're worried about me hurting them?"

I shake my head. "I'm not worried about you hurting them. I'm worried about you *killing* them."

Nobody says a word after that, not until we get to the doctor.

"What happened?" The doctor rushes forward to look at me.

"She was attacked." Tucker lays me down on the exam table.

"Where does it hurt?" The doctor is a lion shifter. It's hard to tell his age, but by human standards, I'd say he looks like he's in his early to mid-twenties.

I start out by showing him my wrist. It's swollen from where Angela grabbed me and held me. There is a perfect bruise outline of her hand. And then I show him everything else, just because I know my mates won't be satisfied until the doctor has examined every single inch. He even does a few x-rays, which I've never had done before.

In the end, I have some broken ribs, a hairline fracture in my wrist, and a concussion to go along with all my bruises. It's not that bad, though the way my mates act you'd think they just learned that I was dying or something.

"It's not even that bad." I pout as Levi carries me from the doctor's office toward our room.

I hear both Mateo and Tucker growl. Even Levi's eyes flash yellow. I can't see Kai to know how he reacted, but I'd definitely say that I said the wrong thing again.

"Don't say things like that." Levi's eyes slowly fade from yellow to blue. "When you do, it just reminds us how truly awful your old pride was."

Ah, yeah, I guess I can understand that.

My mates hate the fact that they weren't there to protect me from their abuse back then. But how could they have known? Fate had us meet at the perfect time.

"I promise I'm okay." My voice comes out stronger than it did earlier. "I'm already healing. I'm not going to let them win, okay? I want to show everybody in the pack that I'm stronger than I look."

"I will make you stronger. We're going to train more often," Mateo declares.

I grin, because that is *exactly* what I want. I want to train more so problems like today aren't a thing. I want to be strong enough to fight back. Instead, today I stood there, and

I let them kick and hit me because I didn't know how to stop it. The only thing I know how to do is take a beating. I want that to change.

"I want to be strong." I make a muscle with my arm.

The guys chuckle, which relaxes me a little more.

I don't want them upset.

When we get to the room, Levi lays me down on the soft mattress. He and Kai climb beside me. I snuggle between the two of them, closing my eyes. The concussion has made me tired. Taking a nap wouldn't be so bad.

Kai leans forward and gently kisses me on the side of my swollen cheek. I smile, but don't open my eyes. I drift off to sleep easily, vaguely aware that Tucker and Mateo are in a heated discussion about something.

Still unwanted.

I wake up around ten o'clock that night. I'm wide awake. Mateo and Tucker are watching something on TV. Kai and Levi are both asleep beside me. As I stare up at the ceiling, listening to the quiet sounds coming from the television, my mind keeps racing. I think that's why I woke up. Because I'm worried.

I am trying not to get down about everything that's happened, but it's hard.

I thought things would be different when I joined Mateo's pack, but they're not. They are the same as they always were. I'm still the unwanted runt. Only now, I guess I'm the unwanted slut. I'm still a runt, they just think I'm some kind of witch who cast a spell on their alpha and three other guys to get them to fall in love with me.

The idea is laughable. Everybody knows that witches and shifters can't have babies together, unless they were mated. Which has *never* happened. It would be like... mating with a human.

I guess there is one different thing since I joined Mateo's pack, and that is I'm not alone anymore. I have Mateo. I have Tucker, Levi, and Kai. They will protect me.

But aside from Mateo and I, we're all in different packs and prides. I don't like that. I want us all to be together. But how can we be? We're all different species, and we all belong with our own kind.

Except me, I guess. The panthers don't want me, so I got pawned off on the bears.

There is a burning sensation in my chest, and it takes me a few seconds to realize that the feeling isn't mine. It's Mateo's. I look over at him on the couch. He and Tucker are talking about something while the movie plays. But a vein in Mateo's neck pops out slightly, and his face is red. His hands are balled into fists, and his knuckles are white.

I sigh, slowly getting out of bed. I don't want to wake Kai or Levi. But as soon as I get out of bed, Levi rolls into the spot I was in and throws his arm around Kai.

Cute.

I wish I could take a picture.

"What are you doing up?" Tucker comes to stand in front of me, his eyes scanning over my body. He's probably trying to see how much I've healed.

I imagine that a lot of my bruises are gone. Since I've started eating more, my body heals itself much faster. I already feel loads better. My wrist hardly aches at all. But my back and ribs still hurt quite a bit.

My stomach growls loudly, reminding me that I didn't eat dinner. We came back to the room and I fell asleep right away.

Tucker chuckles. "Are you hungry?"

I nod.

Since coming to the school, I find that my appetite has gotten a lot bigger. Mostly thanks to Mateo force feeding me.

Mateo stands up from the couch. "I'll go get something for you to eat."

He rushes from the room, leaving me there with Tucker.

Tucker grabs my hand, pulling me over to the couch. I go to sit down, but he pulls me into his lap. I like sitting on the laps of my mates. It makes my stomach tighten and heart race.

I trace a finger along his forehead and down his cheek. I want to memorize every detail about his face.

Tucker is perfect. I've always thought so from the moment we met. When he stepped out of his Jeep that day, I was scared. But he showed me such kindness that I had never experienced before. He gave me hope. If I had known then what I know now, I would've marched right up to him and kissed him. I wouldn't have been afraid.

But then again, I was a different girl back then. I was broken. Even more broken than I am now. My mates have slowly been putting the pieces of me back together.

"He's mad, huh?" I chew on my lip as I continue to trace lines onto his face.

"Yeah." Tucker's voice is rough. I notice his shoulders are tight too.

I feel a familiar burning sensation in my chest. "You're mad too?"

He nods. "I'm furious. I want to steal you away from Mateo's pack."

I grin. "I'd almost let you, but I don't want to hurt Mateo. His pack... they don't like me. I'm so different from them. They're all so... big."

"I'm sorry." Tucker lowers his head. "The second I felt your panic, I came running. But I'm always too slow—always too late."

I put my hands on his shoulders, turning in his lap so that I am facing him fully, my legs straddled over his. "Hey, none of that, okay? What those girls did was *not* your fault."

"Girls, huh?" He smirks. "That narrows it down."

I sigh. "I will tell you guys who did it, but only after you calm down. I don't want you to kill them."

"I know." He reaches a hand out, grabbing onto a piece of my hair, playing with the end. "We know who it was,

Layla. The second you went to sleep, Mateo left and forced his pack to tell him."

My eyes widen at his confession. "Did he kill them?"

"No." He shakes his head. "He wanted to. I want to. But he wants to honor your wishes. He is going to give them a trial. It's more than they deserve."

A trial?

I've never heard of that before. Usually, when somebody does something wrong, the alpha of the pack or pride will be the judge, jury, and executioner. At least, that is how it was in my pride.

"Are they going to get kicked out of the pack for what they did to me?" Because Mateo threatened to kick them out of the pack once when they were just mean to me. Now that they've actually attacked me...

"I don't know." Tucker shrugs one shoulder. "But I hope they do."

I don't.

I don't want anybody else to get kicked out of their own pack for me. Not even Brittany and Angela.

"They're eighteen, Tucker. They don't deserve to be forced onto the streets for being cruel. They haven't even lived yet. They don't know how awful their actions truly were." I don't know why, but I feel like I have to defend them.

"You know." He cups his hands on the side of my face. "You say that they're only kids, but they're *our age*, Layla.

You and I know the difference between right and wrong, and so should they."

I know there is no point in arguing. Tucker has already made up his mind. But I think he's wrong. Everybody matures at different speeds.

"Maybe this trial will be all it takes for them to know the severity of the problem." Because if I were facing what they are, I'd be scared to death.

"Maybe."

As mad as Tucker is, I know that Mateo has got to be even angrier. It's *his* pack that attacked me, and he's the future alpha. I'm sure he feels responsible. I will have to make sure I let him know that I don't blame him. Everything he's done for me has been incredible. He's welcomed me into his pack with open arms, and he's given me a life I've never dared to dream about, but always wanted. He's given me *everything*. A couple of mean girls don't change that.

"Do people really think I put a spell on you guys?" I look down at my hands that I have laid on his chest to avoid making eye contact. My stomach aches as I wait for him to respond.

"What do you mean? A spell?" He nudges my chin. "I have no idea what you're talking about."

"Brittany and Angela think that I somehow cast a spell on you and the guys. Because how else would all four of you have me as a mate. I'm nobody—a runt." I lick my lips. "I'm sorry you're stuck with me."

"I thought you were over that," Tucker growls. "Those girls are jealous that you have Mateo. They are power hungry. They wanted to mate with Mateo because of his power, not because they like him as a person. Don't let shallow girls like them make you doubt the bond you share with us."

I nod.

He's right.

"I'm sorry. I don't doubt our bonds." I lean forward, kissing him on the cheek. "I love you, Tucker."

"I love you too." He tightens his arms around me and leans forward, capturing my lips.

That is how we stay until Mateo comes back with the food.

Tuesday, September 13

Sick day.

The guys have decided that I am not going to school today. They think I need an extra day to heal—I don't. But since they won't let me go to school, I won't let them go either. We're all taking a sick day.

I hardly hurt at all this morning. My bruises are all healed up, my wrist is better. I have a very slight ache in my head, and my ribs still ache when I take a deep breath, but other than that, I feel incredible.

Still, the guys can feel my pain through our mate bond. Enough that they think I'm 'too sick' for school. Whatever.

If they're this protective before we even complete the mate bond, I can't imagine how they will be once it's completed. They'll be in my head and nothing will be hidden from them. But then again, if they were in my head now, they'd know I definitely feel well enough for school today.

I still wish Mateo hadn't turned me down when I told him I wanted to complete our bond. My chest aches when I think about it, so I push the thought away, not wanting to rehash it. Mateo and I talked through it, and we've come to a sort of agreement. And by agreement, I mean we've agreed to disagree.

"I'm bored," I complain.

"Better to be bored than to be in pain all day." Levi gives me a pointed look.

I roll my eyes. "I wouldn't have been in pain."

"Your ribs are hurting more than you're letting on," Kai states. "You keep shifting positions. When you sit up right, the pain is worse. So sitting in a desk all day would've been really uncomfortable."

Okay, *maybe* he's right.

I stick out my tongue at him. "Fine. Whatever. Make me your prisoner."

"What's going to happen with the girls who attacked her?" Levi turns his attention to Mateo. "Are you going to take care of them?"

Mateo's face turns red and his eyes flash black for a moment. "No. There is going to be a trial. I don't want to do a trial, but we're doing it for Layla. Dad thinks it's best, because a trial will show the rest of the pack that we're not just taking Layla's side without giving Brittany and Angela a fair chance."

"A fair chance? They beat her. The proper punishment is *death.*" Levi grunts, not happy.

"I like the idea of a trial." I walk over to the couch, sitting between Kai and Tucker. I pull my knees up to my chest, hugging them against me.

Tucker reaches over and pats my head. "That's because you're too nice."

I push his hand away. "Somebody has to be nice. You guys are a bunch of animals."

They chuckle.

"Hey, not me." Kai turns toward me. "I am fae, remember? I definitely don't turn into a large animal."

"My panther is pretty small," I inform him. "So I technically don't turn into a large animal either."

I realize that none of my mates have ever seen my panther. They really didn't want me to shift because I was starved for so long. It would take me days to recover from a shift. Now, I think shifting would feel good.

Kai grins. "I like that you're small."

"I like that you're small too." Mateo grabs the chair at the desk, bringing it closer to us, and sits down. "I always thought something was wrong with me because I wasn't attracted to any of the girls in my pack. All the other guys in my pack dated girls, and girls *wanted* to date me. But the thought of it always made my skin crawl."

I like that. Mateo was waiting for me. I think it's sweet.

"Tomorrow, we're going to start getting serious about your training. I meant what I said last night." Mateo narrows his eyes, looking at me. "I'm not going to leave you alone long enough for it to be a problem in the future. I thought having Zoey with you would be enough."

"It wasn't Zoey's fault. The teacher wanted to talk to her about something." I shrug. "It's not a big deal."

"It is a big deal." Tucker squeezes my thigh with his hand. "You were beaten, Layla. And I know that might have been normal in your pride, but it's not normal."

"My pack doesn't tolerate bullying." Mateo growls out the words. "From now on, you'll be coming back here to shower after gym."

I should have expected that.

I don't mind anyway, because I always felt uncomfortable showering with the rest of the pack. Angela and Brittany have been the only ones that have been hateful to me, but the rest of the pack doesn't go out of their way to talk to me. They kind of keep to themselves, not that I blame them. It must be weird having a new girl join their pack, especially when that girl is a different species.

"I'm okay with spending more time with all of you." If that is supposed to be some sort of punishment, I will gladly take it.

"Once you learn how to protect yourself, I promise we will back off on being so overprotective." Levi comes and sits down on the floor beside Mateo. "I feel like we're acting like a bunch of overprotective assholes, but we're only doing this because of what happened."

I laugh. "No, I get it. I would do the same thing if our roles were reversed. All of this just motivates me to work harder so I'm not a burden to all of you anymore."

"You're not a burden. Never." Kai grabs onto my hand. "Spending all my time with you isn't a bad thing, Layla. I wish I could spend every waking moment with you, but then you'd get sick of me."

"Hardly." I shake my head. As if I could ever get sick of my mates. "I just worry that you guys will think I'm weak. And I *know* I am, but I'm trying not to be anymore."

Tucker pulls me into his lap. "I've told you before, Layla, you're not weak. You're the opposite of weak. I've never met anybody as strong as you are. The things you've survived... it just proves you're the strongest of us all."

I don't know about *that*, but I can feel the truth in Tucker's words. He really feels that way.

It blows my mind to get a glimpse into how my mates see me. It's so different than how I see myself. I'm excited for when we complete our mate bond. They will be able to know my thoughts, but I will also be able to know theirs. I imagine their thoughts are beautiful. How could they not be?

No matter how bleak things may seem, my mates are the light at the end of the tunnel. Always.

The worst timing.

Around noon, my stomach starts growling, so the guys get up to get lunch for us. Levi stays behind with me to hang out. I try and tell the guys I'm well enough to walk to the dining hall and eat, but they won't hear it.

The truth is, I'm glad I'm staying in my room. As much as I don't want to admit it, I'm not ready to face Brittany and Angela yet. I'm not ready to face anybody yet. I'm embarrassed by what happened, and I am hurt. Not physically. The physical pain I can handle. But I hurt because I feel so unwanted. No matter where I am, it seems like nobody, other than my mates, wants me. That kind of sucks.

"What's caused this frown?" Levi gently runs his thumb over my lips. "I don't like it when you're sad."

I try to smile, I do. But I've been putting on this happy face so Mateo doesn't go and kill Brittany and Angela. I'm tired of faking.

A tear rolls down my cheek. "Why does nobody want me?"

"What are you talking about?" Levi pulls me into his lap. "I want you. Kai, Tucker, and Mateo want you."

I shake my head. "Mateo doesn't want me." He pushed me away when I wanted to complete the mate bond. "But that's not even what I'm talking about. I mean, the pride that I grew up in hated me for seemingly no reason. They beat me and picked on me. They said it was because I was ugly and small. I thought that when I joined Mateo's pack, things would be different. But they hate me too."

"Don't let the actions of two girls get you down. The rest of the pack doesn't feel that way." Levi gently wipes away my tears. "They attacked you because they're jealous."

I sniff. "I would be jealous. If I were them, I mean. Because you guys are so incredible."

He smiles. "Layla, *you* are incredible."

I don't know about that.

"What if we started our own pride?" Levi asks. "You, me, and the rest of the guys."

I shake my head. "We can't do that. Mateo is alpha."

He shrugs. "So. Zoey can be alpha instead."

I lean into him. "That's sweet, Levi. But I don't think we can do that."

I wish we could. That does sound nice.

"I don't want us all to be in different packs and prides. It doesn't feel right." I chew on my bottom lip.

"It doesn't," he agrees. "When we're older, maybe the rest of us can join Mateo's pack."

"I can't ask that of you guys." Because I know that Levi loves his pride. His alpha is a good one. And he has friends—family. He can't just give that up for me. It wouldn't be right.

"I want to anyway." Levi tightens his arms around me. "I never want to be apart from you. I want to run with you on the full moon."

That does sound fun.

I've never got to shift and run with anybody before, but I've always wanted to.

"Hey, Levi." I pull back a little so I can look him in the eyes.

"Yeah?" He looks at me, raising an eyebrow.

I lick my lips, which are suddenly feeling very dry. My heart pounds fast, and my stomach is in knots. "I love you."

I've told Tucker and Kai already. Well, Tucker told me. And once I admitted how I felt about him, I started to realize how I feel about all of my mates.

I love them all. Each and every one of them. With all of my heart.

Saying the words to Levi makes my heart soar. And even though my hand is shaking as I wait for him to respond, I know that I did the right thing. I was honest with him, and that feels amazing.

Levi gently reaches a hand up, cupping the side of my face. "Layla, I love you too, more than words can express."

Lucky for him, we don't need words.

I lean forward, and Levi meets me halfway. His lips press against mine, and we kiss.

Each one of my mates kisses me differently, and I love the differences. Levi is so gentle, but firm at the same time. He makes my heart race, and my body turn to mush.

I throb as I grind my hips against his. He moans against my lips, kissing me harder.

I realize in that moment that I am ready. I want to complete my mate bond with Levi. And judging by the way he reacts, he feels the same way.

Levi doesn't ask permission, which I like. I don't want my mates to ask permission. They already have it. If I don't like something, I would stop it.

He brushes his hands over my nipples. I'm only wearing a shirt. It's Mateo's shirt, so it practically swallows me. It looks more like a dress. But there are still too many layers between us. I grab Levi's hand, putting it under my shirt, right on my boob. He freezes for a second, like he's shocked that I just did that, but he quickly regains his composure. His finger continues to rub against me gently. I let out a gasp as he breaks our kiss.

I had no idea that you could have so much fun without even mating. Nobody in my pride told me about this. I've read about it in books, of course. But I always thought maybe sex was overhyped. I get it now. All of this is incredible. The kissing. The touching. It only makes me excited to get to the real thing.

I want it all with my mates. I'm tired of holding back.

Levi gently pinches my nipple and I squirm in his lap.

"Levi, I'm throbbing." I can hardly recognize my own voice. I sound so out of breath and I'm practically begging Levi to do... something.

He groans. "You're killing me." He puts his nose to my neck and breathes in. "You smell so good."

I know that Levi can smell my arousal, but I don't care. A few weeks ago, this would have embarrassed me. Now I like that he can smell just what he does to me.

"I want you to be mine. I want to complete our bond." I whisper the words because I don't think I could talk loud right now if I tried.

His hand slowly trails down, going just beneath the band of my underwear. He is inches away from touching me where I am throbbing when the door swings open.

Kai walks in first, followed by Tucker and Mateo. Levi picks me up, sitting me on the couch beside him before I can even blink. I don't think I've ever seen him move so fast.

Tucker sniffs the air, his eyes zeroing in on me, then Levi. "What they hell were you two doing while we were gone?"

Levi's face turns red.

I pout.

They have the worst timing ever. We were just getting to the good part.

"Do you want us to go outside and wait for you to be done?" Kai teases.

I roll my eyes. "Kind of, yeah."

Levi laughs, but his voice sounds rough. When he looks at me, I can still see the heat in them. "You need to eat."

My stomach growls, reminding me that I am still hungry.

But I'm also hungry for something else.

Levi and I *will* finish this later, and I can't wait.

Wednesday, September 14

Trial.

I'm woken up early on Wednesday morning by Mateo. He doesn't give me a reason, he just tells me to get dressed, but not in my school uniform. I quickly get out of bed and get ready for the day. The rest of my mates are all still asleep, so I'm curious *why* Mateo is waking me up so early.

When I come out of the bathroom dressed and ready, Mateo is waiting by the door. He motions me over, and I wordlessly follow him. I wait until we get into the hallway to question him. I don't want to wake up the guys.

"What's going on?" I whisper, as we make our way down the hallway.

"We're having Brittany and Angela's trial," Mateo answers.

I look over at him, raising an eyebrow. "At six o'clock in the morning?"

He nods. "My dad has been at council meetings regarding the whole Alpha George thing, and this is the only free time he has."

Ah, that makes sense.

I didn't realize they were still doing trials for Alpha George. I thought that had already ended. Mateo had to go to quite a few of them. He doesn't now, and I'm grateful for that. I hardly got to see him the week after the alpha challenge, and that sucked.

The 'trial' is being held in a large conference room on the main floor of the castle. There is nothing special about the room. The floor is the same white marble with gold patterns as the rest of the castle. There are high ceilings that go up at least twelve feet, but so do all the other rooms on the first floor.

There is a makeshift stage with folding chairs sitting on it, and seats arranged so that they're looking toward the stage. It's nothing like a courtroom that you'd see in the human world. But then again, we're not human. And this trial is going to be held by Alpha Scott. Ultimately, he will decide if Brittany and Angela should be punished or not.

Alpha Scott takes a seat on the stage. Angela and Brittany are both sitting close to each other with somber expressions on their face. When they notice Mateo and me walk in, they glare at me.

Honestly, I can't believe they'd take the time to glare at me when they're on trial. They could get kicked out of their own pack if that's what Alpha Scott wants to do. I would be scared.

Mateo and I sit down on the opposite side of the aisle from them. He holds onto my hand tightly. It's not just for my comfort, but it's also for *him*. His bear is close to the surface. That much is obvious by the way his eyes keep shifting back and forth between black and chocolate brown. I squeeze his hand, trying to get his thoughts onto more pleasant things.

"Layla, will you please come up." Alpha Scott motions a hand to the chair on the left of him.

I nod, standing up. I wipe my sweaty palms on the front of my skirt before walking forward. My heart is racing and my mouth is suddenly very dry.

"Will you please tell me what happened in the bathroom?" Alpha Scott asks.

I take a deep breath. I really *don't* want to tell him what happened, not in front of Mateo, but I won't disrespect my alpha. So, I tell him everything.

I start off by telling him that Zoey usually goes with me to the bathroom, but that she was held up by the teacher. I tell him how I went to the bathroom, not thinking anything would happen. The bears are my pack now. I had an uneasy feeling, but I brushed it off. Then I told them about Angela and Brittany coming into the shower room. I tell him everything they said, and then when they started slapping, hitting, and kicking me. And then I tell him how they ran off before Mateo got there.

I have the courage to look at Mateo until after I finish the entire story. When I look at him, his eyes are black, and his entire body is trembling from holding back his bear.

"You may sit down. Thank you, Layla." Alpha Scott nods at me.

Next, he calls the doctor to the stand. He gives a list of my injuries, but I focus on Mateo. I want to help calm him down. I don't like seeing him this upset.

I hold onto his hand, caressing his knuckles with my thumb. With my other hand, I gently rub his arm. It takes a bit, but eventually he does stop shaking. His eyes still flash back and forth between black and brown, but there isn't anything I can do about that.

After the doctor is done, he calls Mateo to the stand. I squeeze his hand one last time before he pushes himself up, going to the stand.

"Before I hear from Brittany and Angela, I want to hear what you found when you walked into the bathroom." Alpha Scott keeps his eyes trained on Mateo, his eyebrows drawn together as he watches him.

Mateo begins to shake again, and his voice doesn't sound like him—not fully anyway. He is close to losing control and shifting. "I found Layla on the floor. She was curled up into a little ball, and she was crying. She passed out for a few seconds because of her concussion." He clears his throat. "When she woke up, she was more worried about me. She kept telling me how she had worse from her old pride. But I could tell... it wasn't the physical pain that bothered her. It was the rejection. Her old pride hated her, and now she thinks her new pack hates her too. She feels like she doesn't belong."

How does he know that?

I've been trying so hard to hide that from him. I only told Levi my true feelings.

I shouldn't be surprised that he knows. Of course he does. He knows me so completely and fully.

Mateo steps down from the stand, and that is when Alpha Scott calls Brittany and Angela to the stand. Alpha Scott asks them what happened. And they straight up tell him that a panther doesn't belong in the pack. They don't even seem remorseful over what they did. I am in complete shock. If I were them, I'd be crying on the stand, begging for forgiveness.

Then again, I'm not an evil bitch.

Once they sit down, Alpha Scott turns to Mateo.

"Mateo, what would you have me do with them?" Alpha Scott asks.

"Supernatural Island without chance of ever leaving. I don't want them to ever breathe the same air as Layla again. That is the only punishment I see that fits the crime." His eyes are fully black as he answers.

My mouth falls open as I look at him.

He wants them to spend the rest of their life at Supernatural Island? No, that's too much.

Alpha Scott turns his attention to me. "Layla, what would you want me to do?"

I suck in a breath, cocking my head. "Um... I... uh..." I stumble over my words. "I would forgive them. I just want them to promise to never come near me again."

Alpha Scott nods. "Very different answers from you two."

Mateo puts his arms around my shoulders, pulling me closer. "Layla is a better person than me, and I won't deny that."

Mateo is better than me. What is he even talking about?

Alpha Scott turns his attention to Brittany and Angela, who I have tried very hard to ignore during this trial.

"A compromise. Brittany and Angela, you're on probation for the next ten years. If you get anywhere near Layla or Mateo, you will be kicked out of the pack, and you could possibly face death or a long sentence at Supernatural Island." He looks at Mateo for a moment, then back at the girls. "Do you understand?"

"Yes, Alpha." Both Brittany and Angela bow at Alpha Scott, but as they rise back up, they both glare at me.

I really hope they don't break their probation. Don't they see how mad Mateo is? He is looking for a reason to end them. Do they really value their own lives so little? Or are they delusional and not see?

Still, I try to ignore them, because I won today.

Mateo turns to me, shaking his head. "How are you so nice to everybody, even those who bully you?"

I shrug. "I found out early in life that if you fight back, it only makes the bullying worse. I want to show them kindness, because who knows if they get it from anywhere else."

Mateo leans over and kisses me on the forehead. "You, Layla Rosewood, are the best person I have ever met."

My heart warms.

I sigh, leaning into him. "You are my everything."

Nothing we can do.

After the trial is over, Alpha Scott asks for Mateo and me to stick around for a minute. At first, I think it's just so he can talk to Mateo about something, but I'm surprised when he turns his attention to me.

"How are you doing?" Alpha Scott lets out a breath, shaking his head. "That was intense."

"I'm okay." I smile, trying to show him that I won't let Brittany and Angela get me down.

"I don't tolerate the things that those girls did in my pack. If it weren't for you, there wouldn't have even been a trial. I wanted to kick them out. But I ultimately wanted to leave the decision up to you." He narrows his eyes, looking at Mateo. "I wonder if I made the right decision."

Mateo shakes his head. "I don't know, Dad. It doesn't feel right."

"No, it doesn't. Time will tell, I suppose. But keep an eye on your mate." Alpha Scott turns his attention back to me, offering me a smile. "I want you to know that you are very welcome in our pack. We are happy to have you join us. Please don't let the actions of two teenage girls scare you away."

I won't.

I'm a lot stronger than that.

"I survived the panther pride for eighteen years; I can survive anything." Because Brittany and Angela are nothing compared to my old pride.

"Speaking of your old pride, we have been holding trials and Alpha Council meetings, trying to get him kicked out of his alpha position." Alpha Scott rubs his finger against his forehead. "Things haven't been going well. We can't technically kick him out of his position as alpha. The law protects him against that. I guess our old alphas were a little too thorough when they wrote the treaty. Right now, it looks like the only way to get Alpha George relieved of his duties is for another panther to fight him, but we're not giving up hope."

"Good." I nod, loving that he's trying to help the panthers. They really do need help to get out from under Alpha George's thumb.

"I wish we could do more." Alpha Scott frowns.

I reach over, putting a hand on his forearm. "It's okay, I promise. I know you'll do what you can."

Alpha Scott turns to me, his eyebrows furrowed. "You are an interesting girl, Layla. You will make a fine mate for the future alpha. I'm glad my son has you."

My face grows warm at his compliment as I step back from him, closer to Mateo. "Thank you, sir."

Mateo puts his arm around me, pulling me closer to him. "She is great."

"I've got to get to the Alpha Council meeting. It was lovely seeing you again, as always." Alpha Scott nods at me, then Mateo. "I'll give you an update tonight."

Alpha Scott rushes from the room, probably to get to his meeting on time, so Mateo and I head back to our dorm to get dressed and ready for school.

I notice the time when we walk into the dorm and it's already after eleven o'clock. The trial was longer than I thought it was.

"That wasn't very fun." I grab my uniform from the closet, throwing it neatly over my arm.

"It sucked," Mateo agrees, unbuttoning the top button of his dress shirt.

"I'll get dressed in the bathroom." I turn around and walk in there. Part of me wishes I didn't have to be so modest. He's my mate. What does it matter if we undress in the same room? But Mateo seems dead set against us completing our mate bond.

I kick off the skirt I put on for the trial, and I put on my skirt, dress shirt, and blazer that I am compelled to wear every day for class.

I like the school uniforms. They're kind of cute. And it helps me out, because I don't have to pick out my own clothes. A lot of the girls here hate them. I hear them complain in class. I guess I'm just thankful to have clothes.

I don't know what I would do without my mates. Maybe the school would have provided me with a school uniform, but maybe they wouldn't have. Maybe I would've been the only person in class too poor to afford a uniform. I suppose the money that I brought with me could've bought a uniform, but then I'd have been stuck wearing the same one every day, hoping that I didn't get it dirty. That would have been awful.

Once I am dressed, I quickly brush through my hair, looking at myself in the mirror.

I am a different girl compared to when I came here. I've put on a little bit of weight, so I don't look quite so stick like anymore. I also don't look so sick anymore. I swear my face even has more color and life. Even my hair looks healthier.

But how I look doesn't matter, not really. It's how I *feel* that's important. And I feel incredible. I feel stronger and more confident than I ever have before. I know that I have a long way to go, but I am proud of the woman I am becoming. If only I could go back in time and tell my past self to not give up. I wish I could tell her all the wonderful things that await her in the future. But I suppose it wouldn't make a difference. I'm here now, and I am happy now.

I open the door, walking out of the bathroom. Mateo is fully dressed and waiting for me. His eyes light up as he spots me, and my heart swells.

I got so lucky. My mates are all so incredible. And even though Mateo drives me insane sometimes, I wouldn't want it any other way.

"Are you ready?" he asks.

I push a piece of hair behind my ear, grinning at him. "Yeah, I'm ready."

"Good, cause it's lunch and I'm starving." He puts his hand on the small of my back and leads me from the room.

"You're always starving."

He snorts, patting his rock-hard stomach. "I'm a growing boy."

Growing? Says the boy who is pushing 6'7". "If you get any taller, I'm going to need a ladder to reach you."

He stops walking and puts his hands around my waist, hoisting me in the air. "This works too."

I laugh, gently swatting his arms. "Put me down."

He does, but only after giving me a quick kiss on the lips first.

Mateo may be complicated, but I wouldn't want him to be any other way.

Death was an option.

When Mateo and I walk into the dining hall, it's already packed. Our free period is almost half over. The room goes completely silent as Mateo and I come inside, and everybody looks up at us. I cast a curious glance from the crowd to Mateo, wondering why everybody is looking now.

When I first got here, everybody stared. They were curious why a panther was hanging out with a bear, a wolf, a tiger, and a fae. But now, everybody is used to it. They know we're mates, and it's old news. The stares have stopped, and the school gossips have found somebody else to talk about.

Mateo puts a hand on the small of my back, ushering me forward. He walks me to the table with the rest of the guys while he turns to go get us some food.

I sit down between Levi and Tucker. "Why is everybody staring at me?"

"We heard about the trial." Kai puts down his bottle of water, focusing on me. "Are you okay?"

"You heard about the trial?" I raise an eyebrow, wondering how everybody has heard already, even though it *just* happened.

Levi nods. "Alpha Scott made an announcement just a few minutes before you and Mateo walked in. He told us what you did."

"What I did?" I shake my head, genuinely confused *what* I did.

"You showed Brittany and Angela mercy." Tucker shrugs. "It's more than they deserved, and it makes you look really good to the other bears shifters. It shows them that you're not just here to take over the pack."

My jaw drops open as I look between my mates. "Wow. I had no idea. I just didn't want Brittany and Angela to get kicked out of their pack, or for them to be sentenced to Supernatural Island."

"Supernatural Island?" Levi snorts. "Those bitches deserve to *die*. I'm honestly surprised that they made it out alive."

"I would feel better if they were dead," Tucker mumbles. "I can't believe Mateo is still letting them breathe oxygen. I'm even surprised they were alive to go to a trial after we figured out who attacked you."

"Death was really an option?" I rub at the back of my neck, trying to ease some of the tension. "I had no idea."

It seems that if Angela and Brittany knew that, they would've been nicer to me. Do they not fear death? Or even a sentence at Supernatural Island? Or are they so prideful that they can't make themselves even appear remorseful?

"Of course death was an option. You saw what we did to your old pride that attacked you." Kai's eyes turn white for a second, sparks shooting out of his hands at the mere mention of those guys that attacked me.

It was a little different. My pride... they intended to *kill* me. They weren't going to stop. And they hurt me severely. I had a broken back by the time the guys got to me. But Brittany and Angela didn't hurt me nearly as bad. A few bruises, and a few broken bones is nothing.

"If they come at you again, they won't live long enough to get to go Supernatural Island for their crimes, I can promise you that." Tucker growls out the words.

"But you handled yourself with grace." Levi puts his hand on my thigh, squeezing it. "The rest of the bear shifters are impressed. And if you can forgive Brittany and Angela for what they did, then we can try. But if they come near you again, all bets are off."

I highly doubt Brittany and Angela will come anywhere near me again.

My eyes automatically drift to where they always sit in the cafeteria. Their table is full, as it usually is, only they aren't sitting there. I scan the cafeteria and find them sitting in the corner by themselves. They're glaring at me from across the room.

I wonder if their pack forced them from the table. That surprises me. But I can't bring myself to feel bad for the two of them. They did this to themselves.

A tray goes down in front of me with five cheeseburgers on it. I look up as Mateo sits down beside Kai.

"Eat," he demands, using his alpha voice.

My eyes widen as I look at my plate. "I can't eat *five* burgers."

"Eat as much as you can." His voice softens. "We skipped breakfast, and you need to gain your strength back. Healing took a lot out of you."

I nod, knowing he's right.

I pick up one of the burgers, taking a bite. I know I won't be able to eat five, not even close. But I can probably eat two, maybe two and a half.

It was nice to heal faster than normal, and I know I have my good eating habits to thank for that. The kind of injury I sustained would've taken a couple of days to heal from, but I was already getting better within a few hours. It's all thanks to my mates. They take care of me. I hope that someday I will be able to return the favor.

Another tray goes down at the table, so I look over and see Zoey sit down. She is grinning from ear to ear.

"Oh, my gosh, Layla, you are amazing," she squeals.

"Why am I amazing?" I raise an eyebrow, taking another bite of my food.

"Because, you practically begged for my dad to have mercy on Brittany and Angela." She bounces up and down in her seat. "The pack is so impressed with you. We all thought for sure Brittany and Angela would be goners. They deserve it. But you forgave them, which is a very honorable thing to do, especially for their future alpha's mate. They know you'll treat the pack well."

"I didn't do it because of that." I did it because it was the right thing to do, and I stand behind my decision. Brittany and Angela don't deserve to die for being bullies. I'm hoping they'll learn from this mistake and grow. But something in my mind tells me this isn't the last I'll hear from them. I push that thought away, because it's not worth my time. My mates won't leave me alone long enough for Brittany and Angela to be a problem again.

Zoey grins. "Layla, you're so sweet. The pack is lucky to have you."

Mateo growls. "Can we not talk about the trial? I'm still pissed at my dad's ruling, and even more pissed that Brittany and Angela are still breathing."

Zoey lowers her head. "Sorry."

I reach across the table, smacking Mateo's arm gently. "Hey, don't alpha your sister like that."

He pauses to look at me with his burger halfway to his mouth. He raises an eyebrow. "Are you going to stop me?"

I sink back into my seat. "You already know I can't."

I'm not strong enough.

But one day...

Oh, who am I kidding? I could never beat Mateo. He's way too strong.

Mateo sighs, turning to his sister. "Sorry, Zoey."

Zoey giggles.

"Pussy whipped." Levi chuckles, shaking his head.

Mateo glares at Levi. "Oh, and you're not?"

Levi grins, putting his arm behind me. "Oh, I already *know* I am."

My face grows warm, and I try to sink down, wanting to hide myself. "I don't think anybody is pussy whipped. None of you have mated with me, so how could you be."

The guys all burst out laughing, which only makes my face grow warmer.

"So freaking cute." Levi kisses me on the side of my cheek. "Layla, I will gladly mate with you. I'm just waiting on you to say the words."

Levi wants to mate with me?

I don't know why his words surprise me, but they do.

I grin at him. "We can skip class."

"No skipping class," Mateo growls. "You've already skipped enough."

"Your alpha voice doesn't work on me." Levi sticks his tongue out at Mateo.

Zoey rolls her eyes. "Boys."

I'm not skipping class to mate with Levi anyway. I really want to do well in this school, and Mateo is right, I *have* skipped enough already.

I turn to Tucker, who is smiling. "You've got us all wrapped around your finger, and you don't even realize it."

I don't know about *that*, but I do know that the guys care about me more than anybody else has ever before. The feeling is mutual.

I finish up my second burger just as the bell rings. I put a hand to my stomach, not able to eat another bite anyway.

"You gonna eat that?" Tucker nods to my tray.

I push it over to him, and he picks up the burgers, eating them on the way to our next class.

I swear these boys have a bottomless pit in their stomach.

Kai wrinkles his nose as he watches Tucker eat the burgers. "How the hell do they eat that much?"

I shrug, wishing I knew.

Broken promises.

I'm with Mateo in gym class. Brittany and Angela are in this class with us, but they stand as far away from us as possible.

Nobody is talking to them. Before today, those girls were the most popular in the pack. Now, it's like they're pariahs. Part of me wants to feel sorry for them, but then I remember what they did to me in the bathroom. This is what they deserve. They need to feel just a tenth of how they made me feel—like an unwanted pack member.

Mateo is training me again today, and I'm really excited. Right now, he's trying to teach me how to block a punch, which isn't really going well. Probably because Mateo is a lot taller than me. Then again, I guess all the shifters are taller than me.

"You'll get this." Mateo is patient as I fail to block yet another swing.

I am surprised that he is so patient. I thought he would get annoyed with me a lot during training, but he's surprisingly sweet. He's a good teacher. But me... I'm a bad student.

I sigh, getting back into position.

Before Mateo can swing another punch, the door to the gym opens and Mateo stiffens. I look over my shoulder to see Alpha Scott walking over.

I relax my stance, bowing at Alpha Scott.

"No need for that," he says to me, then turns to Mateo. "I need your help."

"Right now? I promised Layla I would start her training today." Mateo frowns.

"Sorry, son." He looks at me. "Sorry, Layla. I have to steal your mate for a few hours."

I nod, turning to Mateo. "It's okay. Go on. We can do this later."

His jaw tightens, but he nods.

"Zoey." Mateo waves his younger sister over.

She runs over, her ponytail swishing behind her. "Sup?"

"Watch Layla for me." Mateo uses his alpha voice. "And do not leave her side unless one of the guys come."

"Of course." Zoey rolls her eyes. "No need to alpha me. I wouldn't leave her anyway. Not again."

Mateo glares at her, but his face softens as he looks at me. "Stay with my sister until the guys come to get you. And no showering in the communal showers without Zoey, okay?"

"I promise." Because I do *not* want a repeat of what happened. Not that I think it'll happen again. Not with the threat of death looming over Angela and Brittany.

Mateo turns and follows Alpha Scott from the gym, and I turn to Zoey.

Zoey is watching her dad and brother leave the gym, a frown of concern on her face. "Something is going on with those two."

I shrug. "I wish I knew what."

But of course the guys never tell me anything. I think they like to hide things from me to protect me, but I wish they could see I'm not as weak as they think I am.

Zoey picks up where Mateo left off in my training. She's not as good of a teacher as Mateo, but I am able to block some of her swings at least.

This is a fairer fight. For one, Zoey is nowhere as big as Mateo, and for two, she's not an alpha. Sure, she has alpha blood running through her veins, but Mateo was *born* to be alpha. He's big and strong. Nobody would stand a chance against him.

"You're pretty good at this," Zoey compliments, as I block another swing.

I laugh. "Not bad for a runt."

Zoey stops, shaking her head. "No, Layla. Not bad, period. Your size doesn't matter when I'm complimenting you."

Her words cause me to lose my breath and I look up at her with wide eyes. "Thank you."

"You're welcome." She gets back into position.

I'm so busy watching Zoey that I don't notice that Brittany and Angela have slowly inched their way closer to us. I'm not worried when I see them standing so close. There is no way they would attack me in a room full of pack members. It wouldn't end well for them. Still, I am a little uncomfortable, just because of how awful they treated me.

Zoey stiffens as she looks over. Her eyes flash black in anger.

"Ignore them," I urge her. "They're not worth the energy."

Angela and Brittany are just a couple of bullies. They are mean to the core, and if they don't change, their life is going to be difficult, if they even live long enough.

In this shifter world, you can't afford to be hateful. If you're rude to the wrong person, they could knock your head clean off without even blinking. Plus, it pays to be nice anyway.

But it's hard to ignore them, because they keep laughing.

I stiffen when I hear the word 'slut' come from Brittany's mouth, but I still don't look their way. I meant what I said to Zoey—they're not worth it.

Zoey growls.

I grab her arm. "It's okay, Zoey. I promise."

They can call me a slut. I know that I'm not. I have four mates who adore me, and when we do mate, it will be beautiful. Having sex with them won't make me a slut.

"They're just jealous that you have four incredible guys." Zoey crosses her arms over her chest, still annoyed.

"I do. My guys are amazing." I sigh, thinking about them.

Zoey grins. "You're in love with them, huh?"

I nod, chewing on my bottom lip.

I haven't told them all yet, but I am so in love.

"It's nice to be loved," I tell her. "I've never been loved before in my life. My mom either died or abandoned me. My dad never wanted anything to do with me. And my pride... well, you see how they are." I shrug. "It's nice to actually feel wanted by somebody."

Zoey grins. "You are very wanted by your mates, and you are wanted by the bear pack."

My heart swells at her words.

I didn't feel very wanted by the bears at first, especially after what Angela and Brittany did. But now? I'm starting to feel like a real pack member. Especially when one of the bigger guys in the pack comes up and forces Brittany and Angela back into the corner of the room, away from me. I offer him a smile of gratitude.

"See, you're wanted." Zoey smiles widely, and I get the feeling that she is proud that I'm a member of her pack.

Zoey is my first real friend. I mean, the guys are my friends. But that's different. They're *guys*. And they're my mates. Zoey is my friend, and I feel like I can talk to her about anything.

Well, maybe not *anything*. She is Mateo's little sister, so I don't want to talk to her about her brother. But anything else feels like it's okay to talk about.

"You know I have to tell Mateo what Brittany said, though. She violated her probation." The smile falls from her face and she gives me a stern look.

"You can't," I protest. "If you do, Mateo will *kill* them, Zoey. They don't deserve to die for calling me a slut. Just let them think what they want to. I don't care what a couple of mean girls have to say about me. They're just jealous, remember?"

She sighs. "Fine. You win. This time. But if it happens again, I will not be holding back."

I nod. "Okay."

That's the only compromise I am going to get, so I give in, letting her win.

Well, technically I won, but still.

Brittany and Angela won't be dying today.

But if they were smart, they'd back off. Once Mateo realizes that they haven't stopped their bullying, it isn't going to end well for them. Not at all.

Completely and utterly beautiful.

That night, I want to put all the negative things behind me. I refuse to think about Brittany and Angela, because they simply aren't worth my time.

Mateo is still in meetings with his dad. He sent me a text earlier to let me know he wouldn't be back until after I was asleep, so he told me to stick with the guys. So demanding, even via text message.

Mateo isn't the only one with plans, though. Tucker's pack is going for a run tonight. He offers to skip, but I tell him he should enjoy his time with his pack mates. I know I've made the right decision when he smiles, revealing his dimples. He's excited about shifting tonight.

I think Tucker needs to shift more often than the rest of my mates. He tends to get restless. After a shift, he is always livelier and more energetic. So I want him to go and have a good time tonight.

Levi also has something going on with his pride. I don't think they're going for a run, but they are hanging out. He also tries to stay behind. Once I reassure him that Kai is more than enough to protect me, he leaves.

Meaning Kai and I are alone.

I hardly ever get alone time with my mates. I do in class, but that hardly counts. I haven't gotten a lot of alone time with Mateo lately, but that is more because of the drama going on in his pack. It hardly counts as 'alone time' if all he's doing is taking me to trials, training me, and taking me to pack parties.

I sigh, sitting on the bed beside Kai. "It's been a long freaking day."

He nods. "It really has."

Was the trial only this morning? It feels like it was days ago, weeks even.

Kai puts his arm around me and pulls me closer to him. I lean into him easily, letting out a sigh.

Being with Kai is easy.

I lace my fingers with his, meeting his gaze.

"I like having you all to myself." He gently traces my hand with his thumb. "I feel like I'm always having to fight for your attention."

I shake my head. "Kai, you don't get it, do you? You *always* have my attention. I'm infatuated with you."

His eyes turn a light shade of pink as he studies me. I already know he loves me. He told me. But seeing it in his eyes still makes my heart swell.

"I love you," I whisper.

He grins. "I love you too."

It's easy to say the words now, and I can feel the power behind his words. I don't know if it's a mate thing or if it's a fae thing, but it makes me feel so warm.

I lean into him. "You know, before meeting you guys, nobody had ever said those words to me before. Nobody has *ever* loved me."

Kai's grip around me tightens. "Well, I will just have to make up for lost time then."

I suck in a breath.

How can Kai make me feel so much?

Before I met my mates, I would've said the mate bond was overhyped. I've seen the mated members in my pride, and none of them seem to like each other very much. But now, I wonder *how*. Because every time I'm with my mates, it's hard to even breathe. They cause my stomach to tighten and my heart to race.

I want to make them *mine*. Officially.

I'm tired of my mates thinking that I am breakable. Kai is the only one who doesn't treat me like I'm made of glass.

I turn to him, licking my lips. "Hey, Kai?"

His gaze narrows in on my lips and his eyes turn a darker shade of pink—lust, I realize. "Hmm?"

The fact that Kai is looking at me like he'd like to devour me definitely gives me the courage I need to say what I have to.

"Make me yours."

His dark pink eyes widen. "What?"

I grin, pulling my shirt over my head. I've never been this brave, but I'm not going to back out now that I've started. "I said, make me yours."

Devour me.

Mate with me.

"Just to clarify, you're ready to complete the bond?" His eyes scan over my face, like he's waiting for a hint of doubt or fear.

"Kai, yes. I'm ready. I want to have sex with you." I lay it on the table clearly, so he can't misunderstand what I am saying.

For a moment, I am worried that he is going to reject me too. Mateo rejected me. He says it's because he doesn't want to hurt me, and maybe it is. But with Kai... he won't hurt me. He's not physically strong like a shifter, and he's not as big as a shifter. He has good control over his fae powers, so he wouldn't hurt me. I know that, and I trust him. I hope he doesn't reject me.

"Are you sure?" He furrows his brows, shaking his head. "I just... you, I mean..." He takes a deep breath. "I'm not a virgin like Mateo and Tucker. I thought maybe you'd want your first time to be with them."

I narrow my eyes. "I don't care that you're not a virgin."

He sucks in a breath. "Layla?"

"Yeah?"

"I'm going to kiss you now."

That is the only warning I get before his lips press against mine.

Kai has kissed me plenty of times before. He's an incredible kisser too. But tonight is different. The way he kisses me, it's like he is wanting to take his time. He is slowly devouring me.

I want him to go faster, but Kai is setting the pace. Even when I try to urge him to kiss me harder, he just keeps going with his lazy kisses.

My heart is racing and my body is throbbing. I'm desperate for him to touch me.

Eventually, I feel Kai unhook my bra, sliding it down my arms. He never breaks the kiss as he discards of it.

He gently traces his fingers down my collar bone and eventually into my cleavage. I'm desperate for something, though I'm not sure what, when finally his fingers graze gently over the top of my nipple. I moan against his lips.

I think this is worse.

Him touching me is only making my body throb even more. I know from experience that this throbbing isn't going to stop until he touches me. But the speed Kai is going, it could take all night.

Well, hopefully not *all* night. Eventually the guys will come back, and I'd rather not have an audience for my first time, even though I'm sure the other guys would *love* that.

He gently pinches my nipples, kissing me softly.

"Kai," I moan against his lips.

"So impatient." He chuckles.

I pout. "You're still fully dressed."

And I still have on underwear.

We should both definitely be naked by now.

"Patience," he whispers, kissing me again.

This time, he does reach for my panties, pushing them off.

Yes. Yes. *This* is what I want.

I don't just want it. I *need* it—more than I need my next breath.

His fingers gently trace my folds, and he touches me like he has all the time in the world. Certainly he knows exactly what he's doing to me right now—he's slowly driving me to the brink of insanity. He circles me and touches me, only to pull away before I come.

I groan. "I am going to murder you if you don't stop teasing me."

He grins. "You would only be more frustrated if you did that, because who would be here to get you off then?"

I glare at him as he presses his lips against mine again.

Finally, he puts two fingers inside of me. I am completely soaking wet, so they slide right in. He pulls back to look at me, a smirk on his face. I'm about to tell him off when his fingers hit right where I've been throbbing all night. All words are forgotten as I come against his hand.

"Kai!" I call out.

His dark pink eyes look at me. He's breathing almost as heavy as mine. "That was the fucking hottest thing I've ever seen."

I pull on the hem of his shirt. "We're not done."

He grins, quickly getting up to take off his clothes. He tosses them to the side, turning his pink eyes on me as he climbs on top of me. I spread my legs wider to make room for him.

Kai isn't the first of my mates that I've seen naked, but he's the first I've gotten to really look at.

Despite the fact that he's only 5'4", he is not *small.* He trains a lot, and it's very evident in his body. But that is *not* what I'm looking at. Instead, I glance down, my eyes widening.

"That is not going to fit inside me," I proclaim.

He laughs. "I promise it will."

I didn't think he would be so… big.

Now I'm nervous.

I tense up a little, but Kai doesn't move to push inside me. Instead, he leans over me and he kisses me again, his finger pinching my nipples. And despite the fact that he just got me off, I am already throbbing again, already wanting more.

"Do you trust me?" he whispers.

I nod, my body relaxing against his.

Slowly, while Kai gently pinches my nipples, he presses himself inside of me.

I wait for the pain to inevitably come. All the girls in the pride talk about how the first time hurts so bad. But there is no pain as he presses in. Just pleasure.

I gasp and he slides the rest of the way in, filling me in ways that I had no idea I could be filled.

"I love you," he mumbles, as he slowly begins to push in and out of me.

"I love you too." But my voice doesn't sound normal. I sound almost… hoarse.

I've never felt anything like this before, and pleasure builds inside of me. But it's different somehow. Not like when my mates use their fingers on me. This… *this* is so much better. How could I ever be satisfied by anything else after this?

Kai moves faster and harder, almost as if he knows exactly what I'm thinking.

"Kai," I say, desperation coloring my tone.

He swells inside of me, pushing me over the edge. I try to call out his name, but even I can't understand my own voice as I come hard. Kai follows, emptying himself inside of me.

It's perfection.

I always thought completing the mate bond was just about the connection, but now I see it's about so much more. It's about pleasure too. And Kai is *really* good at the pleasure part.

Kai chuckles, kissing my forehead.

I raise an eyebrow.

Your thoughts. His voice booms in my head, reminding me that we did just complete the mate bond. He's in my head now, and I'm in his.

It's completely and utterly beautiful.

Thursday, September 15

Cloud nine.

I wake up surrounded by Kai's scent. The smell of our mating still lingers in the air. I smile at the memory, snuggling deeper into Kai's chest.

Last night was perfect. It felt far better than I ever imagined it could, and I find myself wanting to do it again.

I feel a tingling sensation on the back of my neck, so I open my eyes and see that Mateo, Tucker, and Levi are all standing around, their gazes homed in on me. Levi has a smirk on his face, one that tells me my mates can *definitely* smell what happened last night.

My face burns, but I refuse to look away.

So what? I completed my mate bond with Kai. It's nothing to be embarrassed about. If anything, I feel proud of the fact that Kai is officially mine.

I clear my throat, sitting upright. "Clearly Kai and I have mated."

"Clearly." Levi laughs.

Kai stirs beside me. I look over at him and he grins when he opens his eyes and sees me. Now that we've completed our mate bond, I know he's happy because he's woken up beside me. I can literally *feel* how happy I make him. The sensation nearly takes my breath away.

I had no idea how much Kai loved me.

"Good morning." Kai sits up, kissing my shoulder.

The love I feel makes my breath catch. "Hi."

Mateo groans. "I'm an idiot."

Levi and Tucker both laugh.

Kai looks over, as if he's just now noticing the other three guys are standing over us.

"Why are you an idiot?" I turn to Mateo.

"Let's just say I very much regret telling you no." He frowns.

It takes me a moment to realize what he's telling me.

"Oh." I don't know how to react to what he's saying. I wish he hadn't told me no, but if he wasn't ready then it wasn't the right time. Last night with Kai was perfect, so I'm sort of glad Mateo told me no.

"Obviously you're an idiot." Tucker shakes his head at Mateo. "But I told you that a week ago."

Mateo sighs. "I know. I just didn't realize how much it would suck to not go first."

I roll my eyes. "Guys, it doesn't matter who is first."

"It matters a little." Levi grins, letting me know he's joking. But I get the feeling that Mateo isn't joking.

I turn to Mateo, narrowing my eyes. "You told me that you didn't *want* to go first."

"I lied because I didn't want to hurt you." He shrugs a shoulder. "I regret that now."

I groan, falling back onto the bed.

I will *never* understand boys.

Mateo turns and storms out of the room. I hear his heavy footsteps all the way down the hall as he leaves.

I sit back up, worrying my bottom lip between my teeth. "Is he really mad?"

"Not at you." Kai puts his hand over mine. "He's mad at himself."

I blow out a breath, feeling confused.

Mateo is the one who turned me down. Did he really think I was going to wait on him forever? I was ready to complete my bond with him—I still am. He's the one who pushed me away. I won't allow him to make me feel guilty about what happened last night.

"You shouldn't feel guilty." Kai leans over and kisses me on the side of my head. "I'm going to get ready."

I need to as well, but I'm not ready to get up just yet.

I wish he and I could stay in bed all day. I want a repeat of what happened last night.

Kai smirks at me as he walks into the bathroom, letting me know that he definitely read my thoughts.

My face grows warm.

"Why are your cheeks red?" Tucker sits beside me, tracing the side of my face with his fingers.

"Uh..." I lower my head. I'm trying to be brave, but it's a lot harder than it sounds. "I forgot that Kai is in my head now, and I was thinking about... things..."

Levi has a wide smile on his face as he takes a seat on the other side of me. "I am excited for my turn."

I look at him, my heart racing and my mouth dry. "I'm excited as well." I'm tired of waiting. I want to make all four of these boys mine. "I had no idea that mating would feel like *that*. It was the most incredible feeling I've ever experienced."

Levi stands up, adjusting his jeans. "Damn. Now I need a cold shower."

I raise an eyebrow curiously as he walks from the room. I turn to Tucker as the door shuts. "He already showered. Why does he need another shower?"

"Still so innocent." Tucker kisses me on my cheek. "I'm really happy for you and Kai."

I sigh, leaning into him. "I'm ready to complete my bond with you as well."

He grins. "Soon. But now, you've got to get ready. We have school today."

I groan.

School.

I'd much rather stay in this room all day and play with my mates. I've just discovered a very fun, new activity, and I very much want to try it again.

"Shit. Now I need a cold shower." Tucker groans, shaking his head.

Realization dawns on me. "Oh." My cheeks grow warm, and I clear my throat. "I could help you. If you wanted."

He smiles, reaches a hand up to cup my cheek. "Layla, our time will come. I just don't want to have to rush through it. I want to take my time."

Yeah, mating definitely takes time.

"Plus, Kai is in the bathroom and he just shut off the water to his shower. I really don't want an audience." He pauses, cocking his head. "Well, maybe later. But not the first time."

"Is that a possibility?" I grin just thinking about us. "Having more than just one of you there?"

He nods, looking at me with hunger in his eyes. "It is a definite possibility."

I'm very intrigued by the idea of all my mates being there during mating. I don't know how it is going to work, but I'm excited to find out.

The bathroom door opens and Kai walks out, fully clothed and ready for school.

As much as I don't want to get up yet, I force myself up to get a quick shower. It's bad enough that everybody in the entire school is going to be able to smell that Kai and I completed the mate bond last night. I do *not* want to go to class smelling like sex. That would be embarrassing.

Not going to break.

I dread going to gym.

I know that nothing is going to happen, but I still have this fear in my gut every time I think about that class.

Mateo won't let anything happen to me. Brittany and Angela, no matter how much they hate me, won't do anything in front of their future alpha. Probably because they know Mateo would kill them if they tried anything.

It feels good to have somebody so willing to protect me. I've never had that before, and it's a nice change. Before meeting my mates, I lived *every day* in fear. I knew I couldn't fight back. I couldn't even *learn* how to fight back. I wasn't given enough food to train. They kept me just weak enough. Looking back, I think maybe it was on purpose, but I expel the thoughts from my mind. They're not even worth thinking about.

I am still on cloud nine from last night. Completing my mate bond with Kai was... everything. My heart races just thinking about what we did. I hope that we can do it again soon. I want to do that with all of my mates. I want them to be mine.

I can feel Kai, even though he's in a different class than me. If I think about him hard enough, I can feel his heart beating as if it were in my own chest. It's strange, but a good strange.

Mateo cocks his head, looking at me. "You look different."

"I feel different," I breathe out. "I had *no* idea that completing the mate bond would feel like this."

He grins, but his shoulders are tense. "I'm sorry."

"Sorry?" I raise an eyebrow.

We're supposed to be training, but the teacher doesn't typically care if we talk. Especially me. I think he has a soft spot for me. Probably because I was the runt of his old pride, and he knows *exactly* what that meant for me.

Mateo sighs, coming to stand in front of me. "I was wrong."

I never thought I would hear those words come out of Mateo's mouth. I stand there in silence, just processing what he said.

"You were wrong when?" I ask, even though I think I already know the answer.

He narrows his eyes. "You're such a pain in the ass."

I smirk. "But I'm *your* pain in the ass."

He laughs, his shoulders relaxing. "God, I can't even pretend to be mad at you. You're so cute."

I cross my arms over my chest. "I don't want to be cute. I want to be fierce."

"And you will be." He grabs onto my hand. "To clarify, I was wrong to turn you down. I was a complete idiot, and it was the biggest mistake I've ever made. Please forgive me for being so dumb. I promise that I will never turn you down again."

My heart swells at his apology.

It's hard for an alpha to say sorry. I *never* heard the words from my old alpha, even when he screwed up. So the fact that Mateo is saying it to me is a *huge* deal. I don't take it lightly.

I lick my lips. "Mateo, it's okay. I forgive you. I don't understand why you said no. It hurt me really bad at the time. I was ready then, and I'm still ready now. I'm just waiting on you to make the move."

Because no way am I making the first move with him again. Not after last time.

His eyes flash to mine, and he takes a step forward. "Layla..."

I take a step back because we are in gym class.

He growls, letting out his breath in a huff. "We *will* finish this conversation later."

I am definitely okay with that.

Mateo looks behind me, the smile falling from his face. I look back to see what's going on when I see Alpha Scott coming into the room. My shoulders sag in disappointment as I realize that Mateo is about to be called away again, probably going to some kind of Alpha Council meeting.

I hope this isn't going to be the way it always is—him going away to council meetings while I'm left waiting at home for him. I *knew* being mated to an alpha was going to be difficult, but I guess I didn't realize how difficult.

"Layla." Alpha Scott nods at me before turning his attention to Mateo. "Son, I need you again."

Mateo narrows his eyes at his father. "Dad, come on."

"I know. I'm sorry." Alpha Scott lowers his head.

"How would you feel if your dad pulled you away from Mom right when you first met?" Mateo asks.

"I'd be pissed. And you have every right to be, but you know I wouldn't bother you unless it was absolutely necessary." At that, Alpha Scott turns and walks toward the door, leaving me there with Mateo.

Mateo pulls me into his arms, gently kissing the top of my head. "I'm sorry, Layla."

"It's okay," I promise him.

I don't want him to go, but I know it's his duty as alpha. He can't coddle his mate right now. I will be strong, because that's what the alpha's mate has to be.

"Stay with Zoey, okay?" He pulls back, giving me a pointed look. "I don't want to see you in the hospital again. I can't take that."

"I'll be fine," I reassure him, squeezing his arm. "Now, go."

He frowns. "Okay." Mateo turns, waving Zoey over toward us.

She makes her way over. "What's up?"

"Watch Layla," Mateo commands. "Seriously, don't let her out of your sight for even a second, okay?"

Zoey nods. "Don't worry, bro. I got this."

He looks at me one last time before turning away.

Zoey rolls her eyes as he walks away. "Dramatic, much?"

I giggle, shaking my head. Of course Zoey thinks her brother is being dramatic. But it's only because she doesn't know what the mate bond feels like. If she truly knew, she'd know it wasn't dramatic at all.

My chest aches in his absence. It aches in *all* of my mates' absence. I can't wait until we graduate from this place and won't have to be separated from class to class.

Zoey and I finish the class period together. She helps me train. I don't mind her training me. She's not as good as Mateo, but I still feel like I learn a lot. Plus, she's an easier opponent to practice with. She is a lot taller than me, but not nearly as tall and big as Mateo.

She is only fifteen, and she's very tall, maybe 5'10", and super thin. She must've had a growth spurt recently, because it's like the rest of her body is trying to catch up with the change. I am jealous of her height.

As class comes to an end, my stomach tightens as we make our way into the communal shower room. I was going to just go back to my dorm to shower, but I can't let fear control me. Besides, nothing will happen as long as Zoey is with me. I get out of my gym clothes and begin to shower.

"Oh, shoot." Zoey looks around. "I left my bag in the other room."

"Go get it." I currently have shampoo in my hair, so there is no way I can go with her. "I'll be fine."

She shakes her head. "I'll just wait for you to finish."

"It's fine." My stomach tightens as I say the words.

"I promised Mateo." She chews on her lip, but I can tell she's considering it.

"You'll be gone less than a minute," I assure her.

"Fine." She turns and runs from the room, leaving me in there alone. I am a little anxious to be in there without her, but I know I'll be fine. Like she said, it's only a minute.

I hear the door open, and I know it's too soon for her to be back. I look over and tense up as I watch Brittany and Angela walk in.

"Well, well. Look who is here without her bodyguard. It's the panther slut." Brittany chuckles at her own joke.

I ignore her, but my heart races and my hands tremble.

But as they walk closer, their eyes narrowed on me, I can't help it when I flinch. The last time I was in here alone, they hurt me badly. I don't know how much damage they can do before Zoey comes back, but I really don't want to find out.

"You're still under probation. You really want to risk it?" My voice comes out stronger than I thought possibly.

Brittany looks at me, her eyes narrowed. I wait for her to punch me, but she doesn't. I think what I said scared her. But then her hand raises and she slaps me across the face. "Shut up, slut."

Angela spits on me.

I've never been spat on in my life, and I don't like it. I'm glad I'm in the shower.

The slap, I can handle.

Angela spitting on me, I can't.

The door opens.

"Leave!" Zoey yells.

Angela and Brittany both tense, and then turn to leave like the cowards they are.

Zoey drops her bag, walking over to me. She touches my cheek, which is no doubt red. "Your face."

"I'm fine." I cover my cheek with my hand.

She didn't hit *that* hard. The mark will probably be gone within a few minutes.

"You're not fine." She lets out a groan. "Mateo is going to kill me. I knew better than to leave you alone."

"No!" I shout. "Don't tell Mateo, please."

"Layla, I have to."

"No, you don't," I urge. "They didn't even hurt me. But if Mateo knows, he will *kill* them. Just... ignore them. If they come after me again, I promise to tell him. But not now."

She sighs but nods. "Fine. This time. But it's on you. Let the record state that I think those bitches need to die."

"Thank you." I breathe out, relieved that she's going along with me.

I won't allow myself to be alone in here again. There won't be a next time. I'll make sure of it.

Everything I've ever dreamed of.

When I walk out of the shower room, Mateo is waiting for me. I didn't expect for him to be there. Usually when his dad calls him away, he's gone all night. But he's leaning against the wall with his foot propped up and he has his arms crossed over his chest. He's looking around, not really paying attention to anything, but when he hears me step out, he glances over, his eyes focusing on me. He relaxes as he steps forward, a smile on his face. He looks... happy to see me. My heart flutters with excitement, because I feel the same way.

"You okay?" Mateo cocks his head as he looks at me.

I nod. "Totally fine."

He reaches a hand forward, gently caressing my cheek where Brittany slapped me. "Your cheek is red."

I close my hand over his. "You came back."

Mateo doesn't even notice my not-so-subtle subject change. He just smiles, his hand falling to his side. "What my dad needed help with didn't take long."

"Good." Because I am definitely okay with more Mateo time.

"Since I didn't get to spend much time with you today in gym, I thought I could train you now," he offers.

I do want to be trained. It's all I've ever wanted.

I grab a ponytail holder from my bag, pulling my wet hair into a messy bun on top of my head. "I just showered, you know."

Mateo smirks. "Are you afraid of getting dirty?"

It takes me a second to realize he's not just talking about training. Once I secure my hair in place, I look up at him, putting my hands on my hips. "You already know how I feel about that subject. I'm definitely *not* afraid of getting dirty with you."

We talked about it earlier, and I told him that I'm waiting for *him* to make the move. Since I already made the first move and he turned me down it's only fair.

"What is it like?" he asks.

I raise an eyebrow. "What?"

"Completing the mate bond," he clarifies, lowering his head. "I wanted to ask you earlier, but I was so mad at myself. I knew that if I asked you then, it would only make things harder on me."

"Oh." I open my mouth to speak, but it takes a second longer to articulate the words. "It's the best thing I've ever felt in my life." I press a hand to my heart, feeling Kai's beating right alongside mine. "I can literally feel his heart beating in my chest. It's not there physically, of course, but it almost feels like it is."

Mateo's eyes widen. "Wow."

"And when I focus, I can hear is thoughts. Like, right now, I know that he and Levi are currently sparring at the back of the school." I chuckle. "Kai is kicking Levi's butt, and Tucker is laughing so hard. I can almost see it through Kai's eyes."

Mateo grins and takes a step forward. "That's incredible."

I nod, chewing on my bottom lip. "Kai doesn't block me either. He's kept himself open to me since we completed our bond, and I've done the same. I don't want to block Kai out. I like him there."

"You won't block me out when we complete our bond, right?"

"No," I promise.

But I wonder if it's a promise I can keep.

Earlier, when everything happened with Brittany and Angela, I was lucky that Kai was busy. He didn't notice my heart racing. But once I complete my bond with Mateo, Levi, and Tucker too, what are the odds that all four won't notice? All I know is, Brittany and Angela better get their act together before then. I can't keep protecting them.

"I like your hair like that." Mateo looks at the messy bun on the top of my head. "I like seeing your face. You usually hide behind your hair. You're unbelievably beautiful."

I would usually lower my head and let my hair curtain my face, but since it's up right now, I can't do that.

He grins. "I love it when you blush. I hope that never changes."

I brave a glance up and see the wide smile on his face.

"So completing the mate bond isn't overhyped by our parents?" he asks.

I shake my head. "No. It's... everything I've ever dreamed of and more. It's more than just a bond and a connection. It's very... pleasurable."

My face grows warm again.

Mateo visibly swallows, his eyes homed in on me.

"I can't imagine anything would ever feel better physically than *that.*" I can't believe I was brave enough to say the words out loud, but it's the truth. What Kai and I did was amazing.

Mateo take a step back, clearing his throat. "We should train."

We should.

Part of me wants to skip training and drag Mateo to our room. I don't even care if Tucker, Levi, and Kai interrupt. They could join us. But I do need to learn how to protect myself. I can't keep letting Brittany and Angela knock me around when they get me alone, and I definitely can't always have a bodyguard. Learning to fight is my only option, other than them getting sent to Supernatural Island.

Mateo closes his eyes, breathing deeply though his nose. When he opens his eyes, they are black. "God, Layla. I can smell your arousal."

"Sorry." It's not like I can help it. My mates are very attractive and I want them physically. But more than that, the bond wants to be completed. It's *begging* for it. And I am tired of holding back.

The only thing that makes me take a step back from Mateo is the fact that I need to learn how to protect myself.

I'm glad I didn't bring a dress to wear today after training, because I would hate to be stuck working out with Mateo in a dress. Instead, I opted for a pair of shorts. The t-shirt is baggy on me. It's one I stole from Levi. I do that a lot—steal clothes from my mates. I just prefer to wear their clothes. It's more comfortable, and I like smelling like them.

After a few more seconds, Mateo and I begin training. We focus solely on our training, and I try very hard not to think about the fact that I like the way Mateo's muscles move when he's training me. And I definitely am *not* thinking about how sexy he looks when he throws his shirt off. And the bulge I feel when he holds me from behind? Well... that's impossible to ignore.

"Layla," Mateo groans, obviously smelling my arousal again.

"Sorry." I shrug one shoulder.

But I'm not *actually* sorry. I want my mate, and there is nothing wrong with that.

Someday, Mateo will be mine, and I'm excited for that day.

Running with the pack.

That night, after dinner, Mateo is in a particularly good mood. Not that he is normally grumpy... well, okay, maybe a *little*. But it's nice to see him happy.

Before I can even settle in with my other mates, Mateo walks up to me, grabbing my hand. "Do you want to shift?"

"Shift?" I question.

"Tonight, the pack is going for a run together." His smile widens as he explains. "It'll be your first run. It's special."

My heart races at the prospect.

I've never been allowed to run with my pride before, so the fact that Mateo is so excited about me going for a run with them exhilarates me.

"I want to go." My eyes widen as I stand before him. I rub a hand at the base of my throat. "Are you sure, though? I mean... I'm a panther, and you guys are bears."

If I thought I was the runt of my panther pride, it's *nothing* compared to how small I will be next to the bears.

The corner of his mouth turns up on one side. "I am certain. I wouldn't want to go without you."

And that is all it takes for me to be excited.

But then I realize...

For me to go running with the pack, I'm going to have to be naked.

I follow Mateo out of the room, my heart racing and my stomach in knots.

Sure, Mateo has seen me naked before, but that was when I was beaten and covered in bruises. He wasn't looking at me sexually. It was strictly him getting me help. And I'm nervous about him seeing my body.

It was different with Kai. We're both small. Kai probably expected a fae girl to be his mate. He was expecting a girl about my size. But Mateo... He's a bear shifter, and bear shifters are *huge*. Even the females. So what if he is disappointed in my body?

But it's more than just Mateo tonight. His entire pack is going to be stripping down. Though I don't think anybody will pay attention to me, it's still awkward.

"Why are you nervous?" Mateo turns to me raising an eyebrow.

"Uh..." I nearly have to run to keep up with him. "Just the whole stripping down naked in front of your entire pack. I mean, I shower with the girls, but boys don't really see me naked. I wasn't allowed to run with my pride, remember?"

Mateo stops abruptly in front of me and I end up running into his back. I step back, giving him a little room as he turns to face me.

"You will shift before we join the group," Mateo orders.

I chuckle at his command, but I am also relieved. I didn't want to strip down in front of everybody and he's giving me an out.

"We'll go to my secret spot on the beach and you can store your clothes away there."

"Okay. Thanks."

Mateo grabs my hand and starts walking forward again. I still have to run to keep up with him, but my anxiety has calmed down a little bit.

When we head outside, we head toward his secret place on the beach. It's this small building on stilts that overlooks the water. It almost looks like an old lifeguard stand, but it's obviously never been used for lifeguards.

Mateo helps me inside and my heart races as I realize that he's not leaving.

I start to object, but why? He's my mate. Just because I'm insecure about the way I look doesn't mean I need to turn him away. I slowly begin to undress. I pull my shorts off first. Mateo watches very carefully as I slide them down my legs, and I realize I was being silly. Of course Mateo is attracted to my body. I felt his erection during our training session earlier.

I fold my shorts, placing them onto a table. I pull off my shirt next. It's Mateo's shirt and it nearly swallows me, but I love wearing my mate's clothes. I fold it up, putting it on the table. I feel braver as Mateo looks at me. I can see the hunger in his eyes, and I can feel the lust through our bond.

His eyes meet mine as I reach around and unbuckle my bra, slowly pulling it down my arms. He looks at my chest, his eyes turning black.

His bear is close to the surface and it makes me feel good to know that I caused this. I was the one who caused him to lose control. It's because he is attracted to me, and because he wants me.

Last, I reach for my underwear, slowly sliding them down my legs. Even I can smell my own arousal in the air, and I know Mateo will be able to as well. I try not to be embarrassed, because I have no reason to be. I want my mate, and from the way he looks at me, he wants me just as badly.

"We should go." He clears his throat, turning his head.

I grin, knowing that if he kept looking at me, we would stay right here for the rest of the night. And that is *very* tempting, but I also want to run with the pack.

Chills erupt on my skin as I give into my panther and I shift. Usually it takes me a couple of minutes to call her, but tonight she comes right away. I realize that the reason it always took so long is because of the amount of energy it takes to shift. I didn't eat enough. But now that my mates have been feeding me more, shifting is so easy.

I feel exhilarated as I look up at Mateo. He looks at me, raising an eyebrow. "Well, it would be convenient if we had completed the mate bond so I could talk to you now."

Ah, that's right.

I won't be able to communicate with him tonight while we're shifted. Not until we complete our mate bond. That sucks.

I hiss, hoping that he knows what I mean. But how could he. He's not a mind reader.

He laughs. "Yeah, I suppose I shouldn't have turned you down."

Maybe he does know what I'm thinking.

I follow him out of the small room and down the stairs.

When my paws hit the sand, I purr, loving the feel of the warm sand.

I missed this—running on the beach. When my pride was forced to move from our home, I couldn't shift and run on the beach at night anymore.

Running on the beach is always a risk, even at night. But it was a risk I was willing to take. I knew what stretch of the beach humans always stayed away from at night, and I knew how to hide well when I was running. But tonight I won't have to worry about hiding.

I feel so free.

Mateo walks toward where his pack is meeting. In this form I still have to walk fast to keep up with him. I'm excited to run. It's been far too long since my panther got to stretch her legs.

Everybody looks at me as we approach the pack. I can't help but notice that Brittany and Angela are *not* here tonight.

"Thanks for coming everybody. I really wanted everybody here for my mates first run with us." Mateo addresses the pack. "You will notice that Brittany and Angela aren't here, and that is because I told them not to come. After everything that happened, I wanted my mate to have an enjoyable time. I'm sure you all know *why* I did this."

There is a small mumble of voices as everybody looks at one another. I can't hear it all, but I do hear the word probation echoed a lot.

"Let's just enjoy this." Mateo pulls off his shirt and begins to undress and the rest of the pack follows.

I turn away from the rest of the pack, not wanting to see anybody else unclothed, but I do look at Mateo.

He catches me watching as he unbuttons his jeans. He smirks at me. "I guess it is only fair."

If I was in my human form, I would probably roll my eyes at him.

Once his jeans are gone, he turns to me, winks, and kicks off his underwear. I don't see anything as he transforms quickly into his bear. I don't even have time to blink before it happened.

I take a step back.

Holy crap, he's big.

But he's my mate, and I don't have to worry about anything. Mateo would never hurt me.

Another bear comes up behind me. Zoey, I recognize from the smell. Her bear is big too, but not even half as big as Mateo's.

Mateo growls and the pack takes off.

I run between Mateo and Zoey, loving the feel of the sand beneath my paws. I can run faster than any of the bears. Mateo lets me run ahead, but growls if I get too far to let me know to slow down and let them catch up.

We run and we play, which is something I never got to do with my old pride. I realize now how important this is.

I run and pounce on Mateo and he growls, but it's not an angry growl. If I didn't know any better, I'd think he was laughing.

I don't know how long we run, but by the time we're done I feel incredible. I'm not tired like I normally am. I feel good. Amazing, even.

Mateo and the others shift back. I wait for Mateo as he puts on his clothes. Everybody says their goodbye and we head back to where my clothes are waiting. I wait until he closes the door behind us to shift back.

"Oh, my God, Mateo, that was so much fun." I reach for my shirt, but Mateo grabs my arm. I look up at him, wondering what he's doing.

"You were awesome tonight." His voice is low and gravely. "Having you there meant everything to me."

I throw my arms around him. "It meant a lot to me too. Thank you for letting me run with you."

Mateo stiffens slightly, and I realize I am still very naked. He backs up, his eyes slowly scan me from head to toe.

And even though I told him I wouldn't try again, and that I would let him make the first move, I can't seem to help myself.

"You know, it's hardly fair that I'm the only one naked." I grin as I say the words, hoping that they don't offend him.

Is he still going to turn me down out of fear? Does he still think he's going to hurt me?

Mateo takes a step closer to me. "Tonight was perfect, but I can think of something that would make it even better. I just... don't feel like I deserve you. I turned down the gift that you offered me. Why do you even still want me?"

"Mateo, how can you not see?" I ask, shaking my head. "I want nothing more than to tie myself to you in every single way possible. I love you."

He stumbles backward. "You love me?"

I nod, chewing on my lip.

I realize I hadn't told Mateo yet. Not because I don't feel it, it just hadn't come up. But right now is the perfect time to tell him how I feel.

"I love you too." He reaches his hand over, gently caressing my cheek with his thumb. "Layla, I would love nothing more than for us to complete our mate bond right now, if you'll have me."

I can't stop the smile. "It's all I've wanted this whole time."

Mateo steps back a little, pulling at the hem of his shirt. I'm excited as I watch. The last time, I was in my panther form, so I couldn't enjoy it as much. I love the way his muscles move as he tugs off his shirt and tosses it onto the floor.

I can smell my arousal in the air. When I look at Mateo to gauge his reaction, black eyes meet mine, and I know he's just as turned on as I am.

I watch as he unbuttons his jeans and kicks them off onto the pile where his shirt is. I watch carefully as he pulls on the waistband of his underwear. This time, he doesn't shift and I am fully able to see him.

He's already hard, which doesn't surprise me at all. I walk closer to touch him, but he grabs onto my hands too stop me.

"If you touch me now, I won't last very long," he murmurs.

I look up at him, my heart beating too fast and hard in my chest that I know he can hear it. "What are you waiting for, Mateo? I'm yours."

That is all it takes for him to make his move. He steps forward, enveloping me in his arms. He gently lays me onto a blanket that is lying on the floor. If I didn't know any better, I'd think he planned this. Then again, maybe he did.

"You're beautiful," he whispers to me, his eyes slowly memorizing every inch of my body.

He finally touches me. His fingers grazing over my hardened nipple. I gasp, squirming against him. He smirks and I don't have to be in his head to know that he's proud of himself. He likes that he was able to make me gasp like that.

"I can't wait to find out what other kinds of noises you make."

He is careful to keep his weight off of me as he kisses me. His fingers slowly explore my body. I know that he's a virgin because he told me, but he doesn't touch me like he's a virgin. He very much knows exactly what to do. He barely puts his finger on my clit and I nearly come against his hand.

He pulls back a little, looking at me with an intense gaze. "You like that?"

I breathe out. "Very much."

He touches it again, this time applying more pressure as he circles me. I've been throbbing half the night on the verge of an orgasm. Still, it surprises me that I come so fast with only his fingers touching me.

When I open my eyes, Mateo is watching my face with a smile on his own. "I will never grow tired of the sounds you make when you come."

It isn't the first orgasm he's given me with his hand and I know it won't be the last, but I'm very eager to get to the next part.

Mateo flips us over so that I am on top. I straddle him, wondering what he wants me to do.

"I don't want to crush you, so I think you should be on top." His finger grazes against my nipple again and I gasp. I'm already throbbing again, and I am soaked.

I have no idea what I'm doing. I've only mated once, and that was with Kai. He was on top, and so I just followed his lead. But now, I am the one on top. And I have to lead us through this.

I line myself up with Mateo, pushing him in just a little. "Is this good?"

He moans, nodding his head.

I think I like this position, because he's the one making sounds now, and I like it. I slowly lower myself onto him, making us one. I gasp as his hard member fills me. It feels different from this angle, and I definitely feel more powerful. I like the way Mateo's breathing changes as I move myself up and down on him. He hits just the right spot, and I already feel another orgasm building.

Mateo watches me, putting his hands on my hips. He helps me move up and down. We both set a rhythm. My legs begin to shake as I am close to coming again. Mateo must sense it because he grips my hips harder and moves me faster against him.

"Mateo, I'm gonna come again." I nearly yell the words at him as my body moves faster and faster against him.

"Come for me, Layla," Mateo growls.

Seeing him lose control like this is what pushes me over the edge. I come against him literally seconds before he gets his release. I rest against his chest with his softening cock still inside me, and I breathe heavy.

"Wow." He kisses the top of my head. "I can't believe I said no to that."

Me either.

I lift my head, grinning. "You won't say no anymore."

He shakes his head. "Never again."

I grin. "I wouldn't mind doing that again tonight."

Mateo laughs. "I promise we will."

And that is how we spend the rest of our night. Cuddling, making love, and falling asleep in each other's arms.

Friday, September 16

Messy hair, don't care.

I love waking up in Mateo's arms.

I'm naked, but I can't bring myself to care. He's already seen me, so I don't bother trying to hide myself. Plus, he's my mate. He's allowed to look if he wants to. And I know from his thoughts that he *wants* to look. He's very attracted to me.

Mateo leans forward and kisses me on the tip of my nose. "Good morning."

I grin. "Morning."

Mateo sits up, groaning. "I have sand in places where there should *never* be sand."

I giggle, sitting up too. I also have sand all over me as well, but I don't care. My hair is sticking up and I am in desperate need of a shower, but I have never been happier than I am right now. I got to wake up in Kai's arms yesterday and Mateo's today. Tomorrow is still up in the air, but I can't wait to know.

"Your hair is fine," Mateo assures me, reminding me that he is in my head.

"We completed our mate bond last night." I shake my head, like I still can't believe it. Mateo and Kai are both mine. Now I just need to complete my bond with Tucker and Levi. I want to make them *all* mine. I need everybody to know that these beautiful men belong to me.

"Speaking of the others, we should head back. They're probably worried." Mateo stands and begins getting dressed.

I follow his lead. "They're not worried. Kai knows where we were last night. If he didn't, they would've all come looking already."

Mateo grins. "Levi and Tucker are going to be so jealous."

I roll my eyes. "No, they're not."

"Trust me, they will be. I was so jealous when I walked in and knew that you and Kai had completed your bond." Mateo slips his shirt over his head and watches me as I finish getting dressed.

As I slip my shirt over my head, he is thinking about how stupid he was to turn me down when I first wanted to complete our bond. But now that I'm in his head, I can feel that he thought he didn't have a choice. He really thought he was going to hurt me.

I approach him, putting my hand on his forearm. "Hey, that's behind us now. We're mated. You're mine, and I am yours. No going back."

His eyes meet mine and his lips turn up in the corner. "How are you already so good at reading me?"

I smile, not telling him that I could read him even before we completed the mate bond. It's just amplified now.

"Come on. Let's head back so we can shower before breakfast." He grabs onto my hand, pulling me out of the small space where we made love. I hope we come back here often and get some alone time.

The sun is really bright as we walk out the door and down the stairs. It's already warm this morning and I'm itchy from all the places the sand is sticking right now. I can't wait to get back to the room and take a shower. I smell like...

Well, sex.

"You smell good." Mateo pulls me closer as we walk up the path that leads toward the school.

I laugh. "Of course you think I smell good. Your scent is all over me. Everybody is going to know what we did last night."

Well, they'll know we had sex, but they won't know the details.

Last night was amazing. We made love three times before we finally passed out, and each time was better than the last. Mateo is definitely a fast learner, and he seems to really like the sounds I make when I come. I'm a very lucky panther.

Mateo laughs, obviously reading my thoughts.

We walk hand in hand into the castle. Thankfully it's still early, so there aren't people walking about. I'm not *ashamed* of what we did, but I really don't want people giving me weird looks as Mateo and I walk to our room. Sometimes when you're a shifter, you overshare everything. Not because you want to, but because it's obvious.

When Mateo and I walk into the room, Levi, Kai, and Tucker are all there. My face grows warm when I see them. I want to move behind Mateo and hide, but I don't. I'll be brave this time.

I clear my throat. "Who's next?"

The guys all laugh, and Levi jumps up and down.

"Me, me, me!"

I just laugh at him. He knows I was joking. Kind of. It's not like I *planned* last night, just like I didn't plan it with Kai. It just happened, and I think that's the best way it can go.

"Congratulations. I'm only a little jealous." Tucker leans over, kissing me on the cheek. "I'll wait forever if I have to."

I shake my head. "It won't be forever, I promise."

I'm ready now to complete my mate bond with Tucker. He already knows that I love him, and he has expressed the same to me. There is nothing holding me back, other than we have class this morning.

Stupid school. It's always getting in the way of me having fun.

I still have to get a shower. I suppose I could pull Tucker in there with me. I very much like that idea, but I don't want our first time to be quick. I want us to take our time and enjoy it.

Kai laughs. "Tucker, she's thinking some naughty things about you right now."

My eyes widen as I glance at Kai. "How dare you betray me like that?"

Tucker smirks. "Soon, Layla. I promise."

"Soon for me too, right?" Levi raises an eyebrow.

"Trust me, she has plenty of naughty thoughts about you too," Kai reassures him.

My mouth drops open. "Wow. Is nothing a secret around here?"

Levi smacks me on the butt. "Hell, no. Pretty soon I'm going to be in this gorgeous head of yours anyway."

I clear my throat backing away. "I'm going to shower now."

I just wish I weren't showering alone.

I hear Mateo and Kai laugh. Levi asks them why they're laughing, and Kai tells him. Of course he does. But I'm not upset about it. Levi is right. Pretty soon all four of my mates are going to be in my head, and I'm excited for when that happens.

I walk into the bathroom, shutting the door behind me. I don't bother locking it, because I won't object if one or more of my mates decides to join me. I kick off my clothes and get into the shower, washing all the sand off. The bottom of the shower looks like there is mud caked into the cracks of the tile. Gross.

As I shower, I think about how when I first met my mates, I was worried about them being in my head. I thought that if they knew what I was thinking, and if they knew the kind of abuse I experienced in my old pride, they wouldn't want me. I thought they would think I was broken. But that can't be further from the truth. My mates don't care about my past. If anything, they want to kill anybody who has ever hurt me. What more could I ask from my mates?

I am happy. Happier than I ever thought was possible, especially for me.

The guys don't like it when I call myself a runt, and I know that's because my old pride used it as an insult. But I *am* a runt. The difference now is, I don't mind that I'm the runt. Because I'm learning how to fight. I'm trying to become a productive pack member that doesn't have to be watched twenty-four-seven. I am going to learn how to pull my weight. I feel like I'm part of something special.

Last night, when I ran with Mateo's pack, it was the first time I ever felt like I was part of the pack. I didn't feel like an outsider, even though I was clearly different. I'm a panther and they're bears, but they accepted me as one of their own and it felt great.

I literally can't stop smiling, because everything is so good right now. I know that there is still the drama with Brittany and Angela, but I'm not going to let myself stress over that right now. I know things with them will work out. It's just... my life is perfect. I have a pack that doesn't hate me. I have four mates who adore me. I feel like I have a life that I am proud of.

I turn off the water, stepping out. I dry off with my towel, looking at myself in the mirror. I am growing more confident in myself every day. When I came here, I was shy and kept to myself. I was scared to even get a ride with Tucker because I thought he was going to murder me. Now, I realize how silly that was. I was so brainwashed into thinking I was stupid and I was nothing that I couldn't see clearly. Now I do.

My old pride doesn't matter anymore. All that matters now are my mates, and my new pack. I have friends and a family. And for once, I belong. That is something *nobody*, not even Alpha George, or Brittany and Angela, can take away from me.

Life is good.

What is he up to?

When I step out of the bathroom, I expect all of my mates to be waiting there for me. I feel like I hardly saw Kai, Tucker, and Levi at all yesterday, except during class. So when I step out and find Mateo standing there by himself, I stop in my tracks.

Mateo has his eyebrows scrunched, like he's concentrating on something really hard. I try to read his thoughts, but they're blocked. I can feel anger coming off of him. I try to think of everything I thought of in the shower, but I realize I didn't think anything bad. Whoever he is mad at, it's not me.

He looks up and flinches as if he just realized that I was standing there. It isn't like Mateo to be caught off guard by anything.

I hesitantly take a step forward, furrowing my brows. "Are you okay, Mateo?"

He nods. "Yeah. Um… look, we need to talk."

His words cause my heart to stop for a second, and my ears start to ring. "Is everything okay?"

But he doesn't say anything. He just looks down at his hands that are folded in front of him. It's not like him to act like this.

Finally, he looks up, taking a step toward me. "I'm sorry. I didn't mean to scare you."

But the fact that he still isn't telling me what's wrong is what's really scaring me. I reach my hand for his, and I notice it's trembling. My whole body is.

As brave as I try to act, I'm still just a scared runt.

"While you were in the shower, my dad came by." Mateo's face pales as he looks at me with wide eyes. "You know how they've been having trials for Alpha George the past few weeks?"

I nod, holding my breath.

Is he going to tell me that I have to go back to my old pride? Is that why he's so scared?

"No." Mateo growls, pulling me into his arms. "No, Layla. I promise you, you never have to go back there."

I sigh in relief, leaning into his embrace.

That would be a true nightmare. Anything else, I can handle.

"Alpha George requested that you come to the trial today. He's been asking for a while, but my father always turned his request down. But the other alphas… they want to know why he keeps asking for you to come. So, we have to go. I'm sorry, Layla. We don't have a choice." Mateo's eyes fill with tears as he looks at me. "If I could get you out of this, I would."

I've never seen an alpha cry. So the fact that Mateo is on the verge of tears because of me, that says something. He's showing what most alphas consider to be a weakness. But I of all people know that crying doesn't make you weak. I think it makes him even stronger.

"I will go." My voice comes out strong, and I realize that my fear is gone. This is far better than anything that I feared. "We'll find out what Alpha George has to say, and that will be that. I'll never have to see him again."

Mateo gives me a tight nod. "Okay. Change out of your school uniform and into something more appropriate. I'm going to get a shower."

I grab his arm before he can walk away. "Mateo, can the other guys come too? I would feel better if they were there too."

He frowns. "Only alphas are allowed to go. And you today."

My stomach sinks, but I know there is nothing that can be done. I just wish Levi, Kai, and Tucker could be there too.

Still, I will be strong—for Mateo and for the rest of my mates—but more importantly, I will be strong for me. I will walk into that trial today with my head held high. I will show Alpha George exactly the kind of girl that he mistreated.

Mateo turns to go take his shower, so I walk into my closet and take off my school uniform, carefully hanging it up. I pick out a simple, black dress. It's one of the dresses that Tucker's mom sent me.

My heart swells as I think about all the clothes that she sent for me. She must've spent so much money on me. When I talked to her on a video call to thank her for the clothes, she was so happy. I guess part of me expected her to be mad that she had to buy clothes for her son's mate. But she wasn't. She kept saying how happy she is to have a daughter now. And I can't wait to meet her. I can't believe she thinks of me as her *daughter*. It's such an honor.

I smooth my hands over my dress, glancing in the mirror. This dress looks good on me. It fits well, especially now that I've put on some weight. I'm not so thin anymore. My ribs no longer stick out. My face has even filled out some, and I look older. As bad as it sounds, I want Alpha George to be mad at how happy I am. I want him to regret the way he treated me. I want him to see just how strong I really can be.

When I step out of the closet, Mateo is coming out of the bathroom. He's using a towel to dry his hair, and he's only wearing a pair of boxer briefs. The sight of him takes my breath away.

"Wow. You look amazing," Mateo says, looking at my dress.

My face grows warm. "Uh, so do you."

He chuckles. "I'm going to get dressed."

I watch as he walks into the closet. He doesn't bother shutting the door, and I love that he doesn't. I love that this is how we are now. It's how I want to be with *all* my mates.

I'm comfortable with all of them, but I want to stop being so embarrassed about everything. I want to have sex with my mates and not blush when the rest of them find out. I want to mate with more than one of them in the room. Eventually that is going to happen, right? We're not just going to kick everybody out any time I want to mate. It just doesn't make sense to do that.

Levi has joked about watching, but I wonder if that could happen.

Mateo groans. "Layla, your thoughts are killing me. I don't want to go to the trial with a freaking boner."

I furrow my brows. "You want me to take care of it for you?" It seems like an odd thing for him to want to mate before we go to trial, especially considering we just got done showering. I really don't want to have to fix my hair again, but mating does sound nice.

Mateo walks out of the closet fully dressed and he kisses me on top of the head. "Please, never change. I love how naive you are. But no, we don't have time to mate before the trial. I wish we did. Honestly, I wish we didn't have to go at all."

Me too. I'd almost rather go another round with Brittany and Angela than go see my old alpha on trial today. But life can't always be happy things. Sometimes, you have to face the hard stuff. At least now I have the promise of happy things to get me by until the hard things pass.

"Your thoughts are so positive." He grins. "It only makes me love you even more."

And I was worried my mates wouldn't want me anymore once they were in my head. I'm glad that's not the case, not at all.

Mateo links our fingers together. "We should get going. It's on the third floor, and Dad told me they're going to wait for us this morning."

I swallow hard.

Oh, gosh.

This is really happening.

Still, I take a deep breath and I hold on tighter to Mateo's hand.

I've been through a lot in my life, and I've faced things a lot harder than this. Facing Alpha George will be fine. It's not like he can attack me in a room full of alphas, especially not with my mate there. He would never do anything to jeopardize his position as alpha.

"I'm ready," I tell Mateo, and I'm surprised that I mean it.

Today, I am going to face Alpha George. I will prove to myself and everybody else that I am not a wimp. I'm strong enough to be an alphas mate. And when this is over, I won't ever have to see my old alpha again.

So, yeah—I'm ready.

A story of a runt.

Alpha George is on the stand when Mateo and I walk into the makeshift courtroom. His entire face lights up when he sees me, and a sickening smile covers his face. My stomach drops.

So much for being brave. My legs are trembling so bad that they give way as Mateo and I are sitting down, and if Mateo didn't have a firm grip on me, I would've fallen into the seat. He sits beside me, putting his arm around me and pulling me close to him. He leans in, smelling my hair and gently stroking my arm. He always knows exactly what I need to feel better.

"Enough with this nonsense." Alpha Scott stands, waving a hand toward the back of the room, where Mateo and I are. "Layla is here, as you requested. Now stop holding the trials up."

Alpha George's sickening smile just widens at Alpha Scott's outburst.

He loves chaos. It's how he runs the pride, through fear, chaos, and straight up abuse.

"What do you have to say about the abuse allegations in your pride?" Alpha Mutatio, the wolf alpha, stands to interrogate Alpha George. "The girl in the back is a prime example. The doctor says her ribs have been broken hundreds of times, at least."

The doctor said that?

I didn't know.

Mateo stiffens beside me, his hand squeezing mine.

I'm guessing this is the first he's hearing about it too.

"Yes, let's talk about Layla, shall we?" Alpha George leans back in his chair, stretching his legs out.

Alpha Mutatio lets out an annoyed huff. "Fine. Say what you need to say, Alpha, and then we will continue this discussion."

I think everybody knows that it's best to just let Alpha George have what he wants. If he doesn't then he will quite literally throw a tantrum.

"It's the story of a runt." Alpha George *laughs* as he says it, like he's proud of himself for calling me a runt in front of all the other alphas, like they can't see how small I am. But he's saying it to belittle me. He's mad that I'm not in his pride anymore for him to push around, so he has to get his kicks where he can.

I squeeze Mateo's hand, knowing that he's seconds away from jumping up and strangling my old alpha. But doing that would just get him into trouble. I remain calm, taking deep breath. I know that if I brush off everything Alpha George says that it'll help calm my mate.

"About nineteen years ago, I was approached by this woman in a bar," Alpha George begins.

The audience gasps, and I realize that it's because he admitted he was 'in a bar.'

"I wasn't drinking, calm down." He rolls his eyes, but I know he's lying.

Alpha George drinks. Everybody in the pride knows it.

"As I was saying," he narrows his eyes, "I was in a bar. I was there to play pool with a couple buddies of mine when a woman approached me."

"How is this relevant?" Alpha Scott puts his hand to his temple, like he's trying to rub away a bad headache.

"Will you stop interrupting me?" Alpha George shakes his head. "We'll be here all fucking day if I can't even finish a damn sentence."

"Everybody, please be quiet. Let's just get this over with," Alpha Mutatio says, his voice coming out in a growl.

It seems like my old alpha can literally get under anybody's skin. He just has the way about him. I should know, because I put up with him as my alpha for eighteen years.

Eighteen.

Miserable.

Years.

"The woman was the sexiest human I had ever seen *in my life*. Gorgeous blonde hair, nice, big tits." He closes his eyes, as if he's savoring the memory.

"Alpha George, we really don't want to hear about your sex life," Alpha Leo, the lion alpha, complains.

Alpha George shoots him an annoyed look. "She was practically *begging* for my cock."

Mateo growls.

What everybody in this room doesn't realize that this story is a classic Alpha George story. He always has sex with human women and then brags about it afterward. Not just humans, but panthers too, anything with a vagina. He's not that picky when it comes to women.

"So I took her back to my house, and we had a wild night. That little minx was a screamer. And I took her four times. She even let me tie her up and take her from behind. I liked her." He grins, shaking his head. "That didn't mean she could stay more than one night. I fully expected to have to have others escort her off pride property the next morning, but she was gone before I even woke up. The perfect woman, really. So I guess that should've been my first clue that something was awry with her. Women are clingy. They usually cry as my men escort them from my house. But she just left while I was fucking sleeping."

I squeeze Mateo's hand, trying to get him to calm down a bit. His shoulders are tense. He smiles at me, but he doesn't relax.

I'm just glad that Alpha George isn't my alpha anymore. This is the last story I'll have to hear about him banging some chick.

"But it turns out, the bitch wasn't even human. She was a fucking witch. Normally, you couldn't pay me to touch a scummy witch, but I had no idea. It was a game for the witches. They would mask their scent and seduce me. I didn't know until much later when I found a basket outside my house." Alpha George wrinkles his nose, shaking his head. "I hear this high-pitched whiney sound and I walk out to see this tiny runt lying in a basket with a note attached to her like I'm some kind of fucking orphanage."

My heart stops.

Is he talking about *me*? Am I the baby?

No. That doesn't even make sense.

I look up, Alpha George's eyes meeting mine. "Then I smelled her. The baby was a panther. I read the note. Turns out the hot chick used some kind of fertility spell and was able to birth my child. Since the child was a panther, not a witch, the woman didn't want her. So she dumped her trash with me."

My mom did that? She didn't even want me?

"No matter how much I hated the baby, I knew I had to do something, even if she was a runt. So I sent her to live with another member of my pride. The guy had recently lost his mate tragically, and I thought having a child to look after would help him mourn." Alpha George shrugs. "Turns out the little runt is just like her bitch mom. Too bad she was my own flesh and blood. She would've been a fun plaything for me and the other guys in the pride. But even I wouldn't stoop that low. So I made sure nobody touched her. Well, at least not sexually. I told them they could beat her as much as they wanted, right up to the brink of death, but I wouldn't let them finish the job. I guess I've got to have some loyalty to my own child."

Tears are running down my face. I don't even bother to hide them from Alpha George.

He's won, and from the smile on his face, I can tell he knows it. This is exactly what he wanted. He wanted me to come in here and he wanted to tell me the truth. It's why he kept it a secret for as long as he did. He knew that if he held onto that information, he could use it when it would hurt me the most.

Really, he deserves a standing ovation for his performance today.

Alpha Scott stands, turning to the back of the court room. "Mateo, get her out of here."

I didn't even notice that I was sobbing at his story. Mateo lifts me into his arms and carries me out of the courtroom. I steal one more glance at Alpha George, who has the most conniving smile on his face while he watches me leave.

Alpha George isn't just my old alpha, but he's my biological father. And my mom didn't want me. Even she knew what a pathetic runt I would become.

He was right. She did throw me away like the garbage I am.

Layla Rosewood—the unwanted runt.

Some things will never change.

Everything I've ever known is a lie.

Mateo barely carries me a few steps out of the trial room when Tucker, Kai, and Levi meet us. I shouldn't be surprised that they felt my pain and came running, but it only makes my chest ache even more. How am I supposed to tell them what happened?

"Put me down," I tell Mateo. He shouldn't be carrying me anyway.

Mateo shakes his head at me, then turns to the guys. "We can't do this here. Back to the dorm."

With me tucked into his chest, he walks toward our dorm. My heart is heavy and my stomach is in knots as I wonder what my mates will even think of me once they know the truth.

Alpha George is a monster, and he's my biological father. His blood runs through my veins. And maybe some part of me is evil like him.

But that's not the worst part.

My mom…

A knot forms in my throat as tears leak from my eyes.

"You have to stop thinking like that, Layla," Mateo growls.

"Is somebody going to clue me in on what's going on?" Levi's voice sounds panicked, so I open my eyes and see that his eyes are glowing yellow. He *never* loses control.

I reach out a hand to touch him, which is hard to do while Mateo is walking.

"Let me have her," Levi commands.

Mateo growls, but does pass me to Levi.

"I can walk." My voice breaks as I say it, and I'm honestly not sure I can walk. My legs feel like noodles right now.

I look up at Levi and see he has tears running down his own face. I reach up a hand to wipe them away. My heart is even heavier, because I know that my own pain is causing my mates to hurt too. This isn't what I want.

But it *is* what Alpha George wants. He wants me and everybody around me to suffer. He was humiliated during the alpha challenge, and he's humiliated now that the other alphas are trying to remove him from his position. He will do anything he can to get revenge and cause as much damage as he can. I know that this is only a taste for what he has planned.

I survived the panther pride for eighteen years. And I didn't survive by burying my head in the sand. I watched and I observed. But there was one thing that always seemed to eat away at my thoughts. The pride didn't hold back. They were never scared to kill another pride member. Yet, all the times I was beaten to the brink of death, they always stopped before finishing the deed. So many times, I prayed they would just finish me so the beatings would stop. Now I know, they held back because of Alpha George's command. Maybe somewhere deep down inside of him, he cares about what happens to me. I *am* his daughter.

Mateo pushes open the door to our room, and Levi carries me inside. I hear the door shut behind us as the rest of my mates follow us inside. I am carefully laid on the bed. It's sweet how gentle they are being with me, but it's not necessary. Even if I am a runt, I'm still a panther shifter. I'm not nearly as breakable as they think I am.

"What happened?" Tucker sits down on the bed beside me, and he pulls me into his arms. I let him, because his embrace is exactly what I need right now.

Mateo runs his fingers through his hair, letting out a sigh. "I should've told my dad no."

"It's not your fault." Levi puts a hand on Mateo's back. "Your alpha gave you a command—you had to listen."

"I had to go," I say, to make Mateo feel better. "Alpha George wouldn't have stopped until he got me into that room. Today, he got exactly what he wanted."

"Your thoughts are so scattered I can't figure out what happened." Kai pinches his bottom lip between his fingers, pacing back and forth.

I sit up a little bit, leaning further into Tucker's embrace. "Mateo, you have to tell them."

I just worry how they will feel once they know the truth. My biological father is a monster, and my biological mother threw me away like garbage.

She dumped her trash with me.

Those words replay in my mind, like a knife stabbing me in the heart.

Tucker groans, feeling my pain. "Somebody tell me what the hell is going on."

"Alpha George is your father?" Kai looks at me, his eyes wide.

I nod as tears roll from my eyes and down my cheeks.

Levi stumbles toward the bed, sitting on the edge. He buries his face in his hands. "Wow."

"That's not even the worst part." My voice breaks, and I hate how weak I sound. I've been working on being stronger, I've even been learning to fight, and *one* confrontation with Alpha George and suddenly I'm back to being a scared little runt.

Tucker tightens his grip around me. "Layla, whatever it is, we can handle it."

"My mom..." I shake my head, wishing it weren't true. "She's not a panther. I mean, obviously Alpha George isn't mated. But she's a witch. After I was born, and she knew I was a panther and not a witch, she dumped me off at Alpha George's house."

Nobody says anything. I think they're all just as stunned as I am.

Witches don't exactly have a good reputation. Shifter Academy doesn't allow them a spot at the school for a reason. They've done truly horrible things over the years to get them banned, and what my mother did is a prime example. She manipulated Alpha George to get pregnant.

"It doesn't even make sense. Why would a witch want to have a baby with a shifter?" Kai looks at the guys for an answer.

"That witch wasn't the first to seduce Alpha George and have his child." Mateo's eyes flash between black and brown as he speaks, his entire body shaking as he holds back his bear. "Apparently if a witch has a child with a shifter, it means the child will be a stronger witch. Since Alpha George is an alpha, I imagine if you were a witch, you'd be pretty strong. But there is a fifty percent chance that child will be a full shifter. And a small chance the kid will be a hybrid."

I suck in a breath, barely able to believe the words.

To think I could've been a hybrid, that would've been the worst fate imaginable.

Hybrids are shunned by most of the supernatural community. There are exceptions, of course. Most hybrids aren't *true* hybrids. Like the fairy queen, she is a hybrid wolf and fae, but she can't shift into a wolf. For the most part, she's fully fae. But the ones who aren't so lucky, the ones who are a true hybrid, they have it rough. They never quite fit into one world, always stuck between two species. A lot of times they are hunted down because other supernaturals think they're too strong. It's not a life I would wish on anybody.

"This can't get out." Levi pushes up from the bed, standing in front of Mateo. "If anybody learns that her mother is a witch, she will be a target. Those chicks from your pack are nothing compared to the bullying that would await her."

He's right.

Nobody would accept me if they knew the truth.

"I'll take care of it. I won't let it get out," Mateo growls.

"Do you guys hate me?" My body is shivering, but not because I'm cold.

"Nothing could ever make me hate you, Layla." Tucker runs his hands gently down my arms. "I promise you, what I just heard doesn't change how I feel about you."

"You can't help who your parents are." Kai sits down in front of Tucker and me. "It wouldn't matter to me, even if you were a witch. You're my mate and I love you."

"What he said." Levi smirks. "You're stuck with me."

Mateo's warm brown eyes look at me, the black is completely gone now. "You're mine, forever."

My mates don't care, so that is something.

But I still can't shake the feeling. I'm an abomination, born from a spell. Everything that I've ever known is a lie. No wonder Alpha George hates me. He was manipulated and seduced. He didn't want children. The fact that I exist must plague him.

I should have never been born. I know that now.

Saturday, September 17

I've been unwanted my whole life.

On Saturday morning, I wake up feeling slightly better than when I went to sleep. I have no idea how we all fit, but somehow all four of my mates lie in bed with me. Though, I'm halfway on top of Levi and Tucker, and poor Kai is halfway hanging off the bed. But none of them wanted to leave me last night, and I didn't want any of them to be anywhere else.

For me, being unwanted isn't a new thing. I've been unwanted my whole life. First by my mother, who dropped me off at my father's house the second she realized I was a shifter and not a witch. Then by my father, who couldn't wait to pawn me off on somebody else. And then by the man who raised me, a man who was mourning the loss of his mate when Alpha George gave me to him and told him to raise me. I can't even blame my dad for hating me like he has. I would hate me too. I'm just a burden he was forced to deal with.

And, of course, I've been very unwelcome in my pride my whole life. They all hated me. I get why now. I always thought Alpha George hated me, but by him saying nobody was allowed to kill me, he painted a big target on me. Alpha George doesn't care about anybody, so him favoring me, a *runt*, was too much for the others to handle.

Knowing about my mom doesn't change anything. She didn't want me. So what? I don't need her, not anymore. I have my mates. And they want me. Judging by Tucker's erection poking me in the butt, I would say he wants me a lot. But it's more than sexual. They love me. Each of them has told me now, and I feel it.

These four boys have stolen my heart. I will admit, it wasn't hard. I've craved love my whole life, and they just offer it to me with no strings attached. I feel like I've won the lottery.

"There are strings attached," Kai mumbles, lifting his head to look over Levi at me.

I raise an eyebrow in question.

"You're stuck with us forever."

"You say it like it's a bad thing." Me being stuck with these boys forever is *not* a bad thing. It's… the best thing that could ever happen. I just worry about them being stuck with me. Bad things seem to follow me.

I used to think it was my pride, that they were the only dark spot in my life. I thought that if I could get away from them somehow, all my troubles would be fixed. But I suppose that's not how life works. And me… I'm a magnet for trouble. I've learned that during the last few weeks. Brittany and Angela are proof of that.

"You're not a magnet for trouble." Kai shakes his head, disapproving of my thoughts.

I know from his thoughts that he means it. His purple eyes watch me carefully. Maybe he's waiting for me to have a breakdown, but I'm not going to. I'm stronger than I look. Last night, I really let what Alpha George said get to me, but I refuse to let it happen again.

"I am." I roll over, careful not to wake the rest of my mates. "But how could I not be when I share blood with Alpha George?"

I can't even be upset about the fact that Alpha George is my father, because that saved my life. I know it did. Even though he pretends not to care, I know he has to care a little bit if he told everybody not to kill me. And of all the abuse that I endured, none of it was sexual. It's a problem within the pride, but nobody ever laid a hand on me in that way. I used to think it was because I was an ugly runt, that is what I was told, but now I know I had the protection of Alpha George. He wouldn't let anybody hurt me like that.

That doesn't excuse the horrible things he's done, I know that. But maybe it does prove that there is at least a little good in him. And maybe that means there is good in me too.

I do get half of my DNA from the man, so I have to hope that there is *some* good in me too.

"You are a good person, Layla Rosewood." Kai reaches a hand over, stroking mine.

I smile at him, knowing that he means the words with his whole heart. I can feel the truth bursting from him.

If anybody would know if I'm good or evil, it's Kai. Not only is he in my head from us completing our mate bond, but he also has his fae powers. He can feel my emotions. I bet he can understand them even better than I can. So I trust him when he says that I'm a good person. I have to trust him.

"It's Saturday," Tucker mumbles from behind me. "It's too early to be awake."

I wiggle my butt closer against him, and he tenses up.

"Layla, I swear…" He curses, getting out of bed.

I look over at his retreating form as he rushes into the bathroom, and then I look at Kai, raising an eyebrow.

Kai chuckles. "He wants to mate."

"Oh." I nod. "I'm ready now. It just… feels like the right time. I know what I want, and I want all four of you to be mine."

"I'm free right now," Levi's sleepy voice says.

I look at him and see that his eyes are now open and he's watching me. The sight of him lying underneath me, his hair all disheveled from sleeping, makes my heart pound faster.

I already knew that I loved him, I knew I loved *all* of them, but knowing that they feel the same after learning who my mother and father are, that only solidifies our love. It makes it eternal. I know that nothing will ever come between us, and I like that.

I feel more movement on the bed behind me, so I roll off Levi's chest and see Mateo just waking up. He's sprawled out over nearly half the bed, which is why the rest of us were so crowded, but I can't be mad when he looks so cute. His eyes light up when he sees me.

"Good morning." He grins at me, revealing dimples.

I love that my mates aren't grumpy in the morning. I thought if any of them would be grumpy, it would be Mateo. Though, I suppose maybe Tucker is a little grumpy. He ran off to the bathroom in a hurry.

"How can I be grumpy when I get to wake up next to you?" Mateo asks.

My breath catches in my throat.

This is why I know fate made the right choice—because nobody is more perfectly suited for me than these four.

Mateo is intimidating as hell. If I had met him any other way, I would've been scared. But I never had a reason to fear him, because I knew he was my mate. Would I have given him a chance if not for the mate bonds? I'd like to say yes, but I don't know. All I do know is that I'm glad it's up to fate to choose who we spend our lives with. I know not everybody shares that sentiment, but how could they not? Fate looks into our very souls and finds the person who is perfect for us. Nothing is left up to chance, and I'm glad.

The bathroom door opens and Tucker walks out. He seems to be faring better than when he ran in. He climbs into bed, squeezing between Mateo and me. I scoot over to allow room for him.

"When we get our own place someday, can we get a bed big enough for all of us? Because this is how I want to wake up every single morning," I admit.

"You can have whatever you want," Kai promises.

Waking up to this everyday sounds like a dream come true. Maybe not in a bed like this—we all need more space. But if the bed were big enough…

"Yes, that is what I want." I dare to admit my desire out loud with my mates.

Last night, I thought Alpha George had won. I thought that I had reverted back to the scared little girl that used to be beaten by her pride members and petrified around her alpha. But how could I be her again when I've changed so much?

No matter what, Alpha George will never win, not when it comes to this. I am free from his pride. Mateo saved me. And I'm not going to let one bad thing ruin the sacrifice my mate made for my freedom. I refuse.

I snuggle into Tucker's chest, listening to the steady beat of his heart with a smile on my face.

Crazy in love.

After my meltdown last night, Levi wants to take me on a date. Well, as much of a 'date' as we can have considering we're on an island that doesn't have hardly anything on it. There are no shops and restaurants. I have heard other students talk about how they're excited because Dean Westwood is trying to get a coffee shop on the island, but that's probably more for her own benefit than the benefit of the students.

The council thinks teenagers should focus on school while we're here. And I get it—I do. But it's so boring here, and everybody gets restless staying in the castle for months at a time, even though we have this gorgeous beach to hangout on.

Levi has an oversized beach towel that he spreads onto the sand. He even brought a picnic basket full of snacks for us to eat.

"You didn't have to go through all this trouble." My eyes widen as he pulls food out of the basket. A lot of cut up fruit in containers. I know the kitchen staff didn't do this for him. They may have provided him with the fruit, but he had to cut it himself.

"It's no trouble. I barely think cutting a watermelon is hard work." He puts the last container out, pulling out a couple of forks.

Levi doesn't realize that people don't just do things like this for me. People don't go out of their way to make a picnic for me—I've *never* had a picnic. Certainly he knows that. I mean, he knows the way my pride treated me.

Then I realize—that's why he's doing this. He wants to make me feel special. He's doing this because of what happened yesterday. He wants to help get my mind off everything.

I lean over, kissing him. He stiffens in surprise, but quickly leans into me, kissing me back. I pull back after only a few seconds because we're by the beach. There isn't anybody paying attention to us, but a lot of people are out enjoying their Saturday. It's been raining like crazy lately, and this is the first day of promised sunshine.

"Thank you." I peer up at him through my lashes. My heart is racing from our brief contact.

Levi gives me his signature smirk, but I can see the heat in his eyes. He's just as affected by me as I am by him.

We begin to eat the fruit he prepared. I'm not really hungry—at least not for food. But I eat anyway because what he did was so sweet. I don't have the heart to tell him. Plus, he'd probably force me to eat anyway.

"Hey, Levi, do you think we can go somewhere more private after this?" I cast my gaze over to him, carefully watching his reaction. "This is nice, but I can't kiss you out here with all these people watching."

His breath hitches and he looks at me. His face turns slightly pink. "It's too tempting to get you alone, Layla. I want to complete the mate bond, and if we're alone—"

"I don't want to wait." My face grows warm as I realize what I just said, but the words are true. I'm done waiting. I want to make Levi mine, and I want all the other shifters to know it too.

He starts to quickly pack away the fruit back into the basket.

I look at him, wondering what he's doing.

He closes the lid, standing to his feet, and he holds out a hand to me.

"What are we doing?" I ask, putting my hand in his.

He easily pulls me to my feet. "You can't expect me to stay here, not after you said that."

My stomach tightens as I realize exactly what he's saying. "You want to complete the mate bond?"

He shakes the sand off the towel, tossing it over his arm. "Hell, yes."

Once Levi has the basket and blanket in hand, I expect him to hold my hand as we walk back toward the castle. Instead, he picks me up and throws me over his shoulder. I squeal at the unexpected movement.

"What are you doing?" I yell as he races back to the castle.

"Running so you don't change your mind."

I laugh, thinking that his worry is completely silly. I am not going to change my mind, not about this. I've been ready for a while, but we just haven't had any time together. Everything has been insane with the whole Brittany and Angela thing, and joining Mateo's pack, and what happened with Alpha George yesterday. If it were up to me, he would already be mine.

"Trust me, I am not going to change my mind." Not ever.

To be honest, I worry about the guys changing their minds. What if they start seeing me like my old pride did? It's my worst fear. I try not to think about it, because it seems futile, but I can't help it sometimes.

Levi doesn't struggle whatsoever as he carries me into the castle and up the stairs. When we get to our room, I'm surprised to find it empty. Mateo, Tucker, and Kai were hanging out here before we left.

"Lock the door," I tell him, as he slams the door shut behind him.

He walks over to the bed, tossing me down. "Don't want an audience?"

I shake my head, but I'm not certain about that. I think it could be fun to try things with my mates, but I want our first time to be special—just for Levi and me.

He smirks, turning to lock the door, and then he walks back to the bed. His hungry eyes scan my body slowly. I'm still fully clothed, so I pull at the hem of my dress, tossing it over my head. Levi's eyes widen at the movement.

"You're so beautiful." He stands there, still staring at me.

"Are you just going to look, or are you going to touch me?" I am desperate to get to the touching part.

"Wow. You're impatient. I wouldn't have guessed." He doesn't make a move to touch me yet though. Instead, he lifts his own shirt from his body. I watch the movement carefully, my stomach in knots at the sight.

Levi is gorgeous. I've always thought so, even though I was scared of him the first time we met. I thought he was going to attack me right there on that boat. I wish I had known then what I know now. Levi isn't capable of hurting somebody, at least not without provocation. He is one of the kindest shifters I've ever met. And he is mine.

He unbuttons his shorts, kicking them from his body as he climbs onto the bed. He's still in his underwear, but so am I.

"We should talk." He sits up beside me, not moving to touch me.

I groan. "No, we shouldn't talk. Our mouths should definitely be occupied with *other* things."

He laughs, shaking his head. "You're incorrigible."

"I've wanted you for a long time. I'm not going to apologize for that." I shrug one shoulder.

"I'm not a virgin," he blurts out.

I furrow my brows. "Uh, neither am I."

He rolls his eyes. "Yeah, but you were with Mateo and Kai. You waited for your mates. I didn't. I've been with other girls."

"I don't care." I mean the words fully.

Kai had been with other girls before me, and it doesn't change how I feel about him. Knowing I won't be Levi's first doesn't change things either. I can't blame him for not waiting. He's attractive, I'm sure many girls have wanted to date him.

"I've never had a girlfriend or anything long term. It was always one-night stands," he explains, running his hands through his hair. "I was young when I lost my virginity, only fourteen. I'm not like Kai, who was with a couple girls during summer break because he was bored. I was impatient. I thought that I wouldn't meet you for hundreds of years, so it wouldn't matter what I did as a teenager. And here you are. I regret all the girls I've been with."

"Are you done?" I ask.

He nods.

I sit up, getting in front of him. "I will say it again because you don't seem to be listening. I don't care who you were with before me. Those girls don't matter. The only thing that matters now is that I'm your last."

His entire face lights up at my words. "God, you're so perfect."

"I'm the daughter of a homicidal maniac. I think I'm the opposite of perfect," I object.

He shakes his head, leaning forward. "I love you, Layla Rosewood."

"Love you too, Levi Young," I say. "Now make love to me."

"Gladly." He doesn't waste another second as he closes the distance between us.

His mouth closes over mine as he traces his fingers down my side. I shiver against him, running my fingers through his hair. I gasp against his mouth as his fingers reach beneath the waistband of my panties, gently pushing them off. I help him kick them away, desperate for there to be nothing between us.

I want to make Levi mine—I'm desperate for his touch. Maybe he's right and I am impatient, but how can I not be when I know what awaits me? I've been wanting to complete my bond with him for so long now.

His fingers sink inside of me and his lips leave mine as he gently kisses my neck. His teeth bite at my skin while his fingers explore me. I am panting uncontrollably, but I'm much too turned on to be embarrassed by it.

I trace my fingers down his abs and stomach, slipping them gently beneath the band of his underwear. I don't really know what I'm doing, but I grab onto his length, gently stroking it. He moans, panting right along with me.

I smile, thinking that he *definitely* likes that.

Levi doesn't let me touch him for long. He pushes me back on the mattress, burying his face between my legs. I'm about to ask him what he's doing when he licks my center and all other thoughts are forgotten.

I have never felt anything like this before in my life. I reach over, fisting the sheets in my hands, crying out at the pleasure. Levi seems pleased by the sounds coming out of my mouth, because his licks become more desperate. My body throbs beneath his touch as an orgasm slowly builds until, finally, I come against his tongue.

"Oh, my God. Levi." I breathe out his name.

He lifts his head a little, smirking at me. "Did you like that?"

Words aren't enough, so I just nod. I don't think I could talk right now if I wanted to. "Can we do that again later?"

"Definitely." He slowly climbs up the bed. "The sounds you make are fucking sexy. But I am nowhere near done with you."

My breath catches in my throat.

This is a side of Levi that I have never seen before, and I like it a lot.

He presses his lips against mine again, and he kisses me. I can taste myself on his tongue.

I feel him align himself with my center. He pauses, not breaking our kiss. But he's giving me time to back out if I want to. There is *no way* that is happening. I thrust my hips forward, urging him to continue. He takes the hint, slowly pushing himself inside of me. Once he pushes all the way inside, he pauses, pulling his head back to look at me.

"You feel incredible," he whispers.

I could say the same thing about him, but he begins to move, and all other thoughts are forgotten. The only thing on my mind is the absolute pleasure that takes my breath away.

This is something I will never grow tired of. Mating is far more fun than I ever imagined it could be.

I feel another orgasm building, and Levi moves against me harder, as if he can read my mind. He's not in my head yet, but soon. I have a feeling he just knows from the sounds I make. I'm definitely not quiet about it as he fills me in the most intimate ways possible.

"Levi," I gasp.

My body spasms beneath him as I go over the edge. I hear Levi call my name as I ride out the wave of pleasure, and his body collapses against mine. He pushes a piece of hair off my face and kisses my forehead so gently.

"You're mine now." His voice is rough and he sounds out of breath. I'm a little out of breath myself.

My chest aches at his beautiful words.

I am his.

He is mine.

Forever.

And this is only the start of our forever.

I'm so crazy in love with Levi Young.

All mine.

Later that night, I lie on the bed with Tucker and Levi. Mateo is off doing some kind of alpha thing, and Kai is working on his homework. I probably should work on mine too, but procrastination is winning tonight.

I hold Tucker's hand as I snuggle into his chest.

He's the only one I haven't completed my mate bond with, though I didn't save him for last on purpose. It just happened to work out that way.

Tucker is the first of my mates that I met. He followed my bus for fifteen hours just to make sure I made it to school safely. He is sweet, but also tough. He's not an alpha, like

Mateo, but he would make a good alpha. He's strong and always puts others first—that is a sign of a good alpha.

I try *not* to think about Alpha George, and how he's the opposite of a good alpha, but it seems I can't help it. He's consumed too much of my thoughts since the trial yesterday.

"Only happy thoughts tonight." Levi rubs his hand on my back, gently caressing me.

I turn my head to look over at him. "I don't think I'll ever get used to sharing what's in my head with the four of you. I feel like you guys are going to always gang up against me."

He smirks. "Only for the benefit of you. I promise any teasing that occurs you will like."

I have a feeling I will like it too.

But as I snuggle into Tucker's chest, I realize that there is still one missing piece. Tucker and I haven't completed our mate bond yet, and I can feel my soul calling out for him. The bond is pushing me to mate with him, not that I need it to. I *want* to complete my bond with Tucker. I am ready.

Kai clears his throat, standing from the couch. "You know, I think I'm going to go out for a couple of hours."

I look over at him, wondering what he's doing.

Levi also stands. "I'll go with you."

"Where are you guys going?" Tucker looks between them, furrowing his brows.

"Have fun." Kai walks out the door first, followed by Levi.

Tucker stares at the closed door for a moment, then turns his head to look at me. "Do you know what they were up to?"

I shake my head.

But then I hear their thoughts and realize they were leaving to give Tucker and me some alone time. They read my thoughts about being ready and didn't want to be in the way. They want me to complete my bond with Tucker.

My face grows warm.

"What is it?" Tucker runs his thumb along my cheek. "Why are you blushing?"

"They left because of me," I admit. "My thoughts."

A few weeks ago, the thought of admitting my feelings out loud like this would be too much. But now… I'm not the same girl. I've survived so much. And completing my bond with Mateo, Levi, and Kai has made me brave. I know what I want, and that's Tucker.

"What were you thinking about?" Tucker's voice is rough and gravely, like he *knows* what I'm about to say.

I look up, meeting his gaze. "I was thinking that I am ready to complete my mate bond with you. I am tired of waiting. I want all four of you to be mine."

And that is the truth.

Tucker, never breaking eye contact, gently runs his finger from my shoulder, over my collarbone, and gently over my cleavage. His finger trails downward. "I've wanted you from the moment I laid eyes on you. That night, when you climbed into my cot, I wanted you then. But I knew you weren't ready then. It killed me to wait."

My breathing grows faster, becoming more audible as his fingers gently caress and explore my body. "I wanted you then, and I still want you now."

But maybe he's right that I wasn't ready then.

Now? Now I am *so* ready.

"I can smell your arousal." Tucker's eyes flash yellow as he looks at me, his eyes glowing in the darkening room. The sun is starting to set outside, but we don't need lights to see. We're shifters.

He leans closer, pressing his body into mine, and kisses me. His teeth drag across my lower lip and he gently nips me. Slowly, his lips trail from my mouth and down my cheek and neck. He kisses my collarbone. My breath hitches as he moves farther down, making the same pattern into my cleavage that his finger did only moments ago.

My dress is in the way. I expect him to pull away so he can take my dress off, but he doesn't. Instead, he rips my dress from my body. I know I should be mad that he ruined my clothes, but instead the act makes my body shiver with anticipation. My panties grow even wetter, and Tucker's yellow eyes meet my brown ones as he smells just how much he is turning me on.

My bra is ripped away, much like my dress, and he continues his exploration of my breasts. I arch my back, trying to get him to kiss me harder. I want him to bite me and mark me. I need him to *devour* me.

"Tucker," I whimper out his name. "Please."

"Please what?" Tucker looks at me, sharply lifting his chin as if he's daring me to admit all the naughty things that I want him to do with my body.

"Don't be gentle. I want you to fuck me." I've never said the f-word out loud before, but during sex it feels liberating to say it. It's exactly what I want from Tucker.

His eyes widen as he looks at me in complete shock. It takes him a moment to process what I am telling him to do. He leans forward and he kisses me—hard this time. He licks and bites and takes everything that he wants, not holding back. I love that he doesn't hold back. He doesn't treat me like I'm a breakable runt.

His grip on my thighs tighten as he slowly kisses his way into my cleavage again. I think Tucker really likes my breasts, so I jut out my chest, urging him on.

"Tucker," I breathe out. "I want you inside me."

He pulls back, his eyes are still yellow as he looks at me. I wouldn't be surprised if my own eyes were yellow, because I can feel my panther close to the surface. Tucker takes no time throwing his shirt and pants off. Once again, he rips the remainder of my clothes from my body. Just a pair of soaked panties, but the action causes me the throb.

Tucker doesn't waste any time aligning himself with my center before he pushes forward. He doesn't take his time. He just thrusts in, and I'm so wet that he doesn't meet any resistance. I gasp as he fills me for the first time.

He throws his head back and moans. "Layla, you're so tight. I don't think I will last long."

I don't think I will last long either, truthfully.

I put my arms around his neck, pulling his lips down to mine. I kiss him hard, urging him to keep going. He moves his finger against my clit as he moves in and out of me with force. I've never been taken like this before, but I like it a lot. I'm so sensitive from all the teasing that I come quickly. Tucker was already halfway there. He empties himself inside of me while I come down from my high.

I can feel my pulse beating around his softening member, and my heart is racing really fast.

"That was incredible, Layla." Tucker pulls back a little so he can look at me, but he doesn't move out of me yet. "But I didn't last nearly long enough. We've got to do that again."

I grin. "I could go another round."

He laughs. "You're insatiable."

I shrug. "I guess I have to be considering I have four mates."

He gently presses his lips against mine. "I love you."

"I love you too."

But it's more than just words now. I can *feel* his love so strongly. I always could, but it's different now. It's on a deeper level.

Scientist's don't understand the mate bond. It's not something that can be studied or explained. It can't be replicated. It just something that *is*. It's something built into our very DNA, and it's magic. I always knew it, in theory, but reading about it and feeling it are two very different things.

Tucker gently trails his fingers down my arms. My arms tingle from the touch, and I shiver. Tucker seems to like that a lot, so he does it again.

"I have always respected the mate bonds, but I thought it was overhyped by mated couples." He shakes his head. "I was wrong. This… I will never grow tired of it. I could make love to you every day for the rest of our lives, and it will never be enough. You are my everything, Layla Rosewood."

"You're mine, Tucker Lewis."

All mine.

I pull his lips back to mine and I kiss him hard. I feel him grow hard inside of me again. And, well, I'm definitely okay with round two.

Sunday, September 18

So complete.

Tucker has me pulled tightly against him as I wake up, and I can't help but smile at my memories of us mating.

Kai and Levi really did give us a *couple* of hours, and Tucker took full advantage of every second they were gone. I had no idea that mating could be like *that*. It was incredible. I have chills just thinking about it.

Mating is unique with every single one of my mates. They each make me feel so good, but so different than the other. My mind does wonder what it would be like to mate with them all, but I push those thoughts aside, not wanting to go there. Not when the guys are in my head. They will all know exactly what I'm thinking, and what I'm thinking is embarrassing.

Tucker shifts a little, turning to face me. "Not embarrassing."

My face warms as I realize that Tucker is awake and is definitely listening to my inner thoughts. I have a feeling my cheeks are going to be permanently pink with these guys listening in on my every thought. I should block them, but I don't want to. I like the idea of them listening to everything.

"I will mate with you any time that you like, even if the other guys join in." He kisses me on the cheek. "You're adorable when you blush."

I groan, hiding my face with my hands.

Tucker pulls me into his arms, chuckling.

I feel different today. I feel… complete. I hadn't realized how different things would be once I completed my mate bond with all four of my mates. And I've always felt like I belonged with them, and I felt good with them, but this is next-level.

I wrap my arms around Tucker, loving how it feels to be held like this. His arms relax a little and I look up to see that he's fallen back to sleep. I smile at the sight of him sleeping.

Tucker doesn't like to get up early. I carefully untangle myself from his arms and crawl off the bed so I can get ready for the day.

I'm glad it's Sunday. I am not looking forward to going back to class on Monday. I know that nobody knows the truth about my parents, but what if they can tell? Even though I am a panther shifter, some part of me, no matter how small, is a witch too. I'm not a true hybrid, but what if somebody smells the difference in me?

I know my thoughts are silly. If my panther pride never figured it out and if nobody at school has figured it out then why would that change just because now I know?

What if Alpha George tells somebody? Or one of the other alphas?

Witches aren't respected in the supernatural community. What happened between my mother and Alpha George is a good example of *why* they're so disliked by everybody. They're typically selfish—they take what they want without remorse or thought of anybody else.

The only thing that makes me feel better is the fact that I know myself. I know that I'm nothing like Alpha George or my mother. I *know* that I am a good person, and knowing that my DNA comes from two evil people doesn't change that.

When I step out of the shower, I am surprised to see Kai standing in the bathroom. Even though we've mated, I am still uncomfortable with being naked in front of anybody. I clear my throat, forcing my arms to stay at my sides. I won't cover myself.

"Kai, what are you doing?" I reach for my towel, wrapping it around me.

"I'm here because your emo thoughts woke me up." He crosses his arms over his chest as he leans against the counter.

I walk past him, grabbing my toothbrush. "Sorry. I'll try to remember to block you next time I decide to have an existential crisis."

Kai smirks, his eyes meeting mine in the mirror. "I had no idea that this sarcastic side of you existed, but I like it. You amuse me."

I roll my eyes as I begin to brush my teeth.

Glad I can 'amuse' Kai. Though I wasn't having an existential crisis to amuse him. It's just something I have to deal with since Alpha George dropped that bomb. Once I work through all the emotions, I'll be fine. But I'm still trying to process the fact that my entire life has been a lie.

"That's not what I meant." Kai takes a step closer to me. "I just want to be close to you right now. I don't like that you're hurting."

That's sweet, actually.

And I'm not really hurting. Not anymore. I'm just… processing. I'm very happy right now. I feel light as a feather. I know that is the result of me completing the bond. I'm whole now.

"We all feel it." Kai's eyes fade from purple to pink. "It's an incredible feeling."

I rinse my mouth out, putting my toothpaste back in the holder, and then I turn to Kai.

"It *is* incredible. I never thought I would have even one mate, let alone four. I'm so overwhelmed right now, I don't even know what to think. But I'm so happy, Kai. Never doubt that." I just worry I don't deserve all this happiness.

Kai takes a step closer to me, his body pressing against the front of my towel. His puts his hands on the side of my head, tangling his fingers in my wet hair. "Layla, you deserve all the happiness in the world. Nobody is more deserving than you are."

My heart warms at his words. I know he only feels that way because he's my mate, but I love that he does feel that way about me.

I lean forward and he meets me halfway, gently kissing me. I sigh, leaning farther into him.

A sudden noise startles me, making me jump as I pull back from Kai. I look over to the source of the noise and find Levi sticking his head inside the bathroom.

"Why didn't I get invited to this party you guys are having?" Levi smirks as he looks between Kai and me.

I ignore him, turning to grab my brush.

"Can I?" Kai asks, motioning toward my brush.

I shrug, handing it over. I hate brushing my hair anyway.

Levi steps farther inside leaning against the doorframe. "So is this what we do now? We stand around and braid each other's hair?"

I stick my tongue out at him. Not the most mature move, but then again, it's Levi. He's not mature either.

"I'll have you know, I am very mature." Levi shoves his hands into the front pockets of his jeans. "I'm disappointed. I thought I was going to get a show."

His words make my center throb, and my face grows warm. I *know* Levi can smell my arousal, and even if he couldn't, he's in my head. He knows what I'm thinking. And I like what he's saying way too much.

His pupils dilate as he looks at me. "We created a monster."

I grin. "I was already a monster, I just didn't know it."

Though I meant the words playfully, I still feel a stab in my chest as I realize how true my words really are. I *am* a monster.

Kai stops brushing my hair, so I turn to face him.

"If you don't stop with the emo thoughts, I am going to spank you," he threatens, holding up the brush.

"I might like that." As soon as the words leave my mouth, I slap a hand over my lips.

I can't believe I just said that.

Kai's eyes turn hot pink as he looks at me, and I can feel the lust coming from him through our mate bond.

Levi chuckles from behind me. "Maybe I'll get a show after all."

I turn back around, glaring at him, and Kai goes back to brushing my hair.

Being mated is liberating. I can say my thoughts out loud without fear of sounding stupid or being made fun of. My mates get me. That is why fate handpicked them for me.

"Never be embarrassed by your desires." Levi takes a step closer and gently rubs his thumb along my cheek.

I chew on the side of my lip, looking up at him. "Thanks, Levi."

I won't be embarrassed—not anymore.

Maybe happiness is possible.

Later that afternoon, I *have* to work on my schoolwork. I've missed so much class and I have a lot to catch up on. I procrastinated all day yesterday and most of the day today, but I have to have this done by tomorrow.

My mates are super distracting, in the best ways possible, so Kai and I head to the library to finish up our work. Well, my work. His homework is done because he doesn't have nearly as much as I do, but my mates still aren't letting me go off on my own. Not that I want to be by myself anyway. Kai makes doing my homework sort of fun.

I used to love doing my homework. Going to school was one of my favorite parts of the day when I lived with my old pride. Maybe because school was my escape. My teachers weren't so bad. They weren't cruel to me and because I was older, I was taught separate from the children in the pride. School was my break from the abuse and suffering, especially when all the kids my age were at Shifter Academy. Summer, however, was always hell.

Kai turns away from my book to look at me. "You're free from them now. There is no need to think about the horrible things they did to you, not anymore. Especially not in front of Mateo, Tucker, and Levi. Shifters are… very angry, I'm learning."

I smile at his words. "I'm a shifter, and I'm not angry."

"Yes, but you are the exception." He taps his finger on the book. "Now, focus."

I groan.

I don't want to focus. I'd much rather use one of the private rooms in the library to mate with Kai. Now *that* sounds fun.

His hot pink eyes flash to mine. "Finish your work first, then we can check out the private rooms.

I groan. "That's cruel, Kai Bennett."

His promise, as cruel as it is, does motivate me to work harder, which is probably what he wanted.

"I hope I don't have to skip school for any more trials." I chew on the end of my pen as I stare vacantly at my textbook. Some of the teachers in this school are old-fashioned and prefer textbooks and pens over iPads, but most of the teachers work electronically now.

"I doubt the Alpha Council will ask you to come to another trial after what happened last time." Kai plays with the end of my hair, his eyes flashing between purple, pink, and blue. "Besides, it's Mateo's right as your alpha to tell them no."

I jerk my head around to look at him. "Alpha Scott is my alpha."

He shakes his head. "No, technically Mateo is. He won the alpha challenge, not Alpha Scott."

I didn't know that. Though, I suppose it doesn't really change anything.

"Should I start calling him Alpha Mateo now?" It's a joke—mates never refer to their bonded with proper titles. It would be weird.

Kai snorts. "Please don't. Mateo has a big enough ego as it is."

Mateo isn't arrogant, at least not in the way Levi is, but he does love to boss us all around. It's just part of being mated to an alpha. Mateo is worth it.

"What is it like to have an alpha?" Kai asks.

I shrug one shoulder. "I suppose it's the same as you having a queen."

"Our queen doesn't order us around. And we don't have fae communities like the shifters do. We used to, but not anymore. We're free to do what we want and live where we want, as long as it's not against the law. We could even live with the humans, as long as we hide our fae features."

That is a lot different than shifters. "The animal within craves a pack. I think my panther would be lonely if I had to go back to shifting on my own." I have no idea how I did it before. "But, since we are all animals within, we have to have some kind of order. It would be chaotic without an alpha. Even one as evil as Alpha George is important."

Kai's lips turn down at the mention of my biological father. "You know, Mateo told us the awful things that he said in the courtroom. I hate that you had to sit there and listen to that. I hope you know that you're not trash, even if your parents thought you were."

I reach over and grab his hand, squeezing it. "I know I'm not trash. Though, sometimes it's hard to remember that. I've been treated that way my whole life. But you guys make everything better. I'm starting to believe that maybe I am better than my old pride told me I was."

"Good. Because you're worth everything to me."

Kai's promise about the private study room plays through my head, so I turn back to my homework to try and get it finished. As I finish up my work, I hear laughter so I look up. Brittany and Angela are standing in the library. I know they can see me from where they stand, but they're not looking at me or even paying attention to me.

This is what I wanted… I just wanted to be left alone to enjoy my new life in the pack. I didn't want to fight anymore. Now, it seems that it's actually happening.

When they beat me, I felt so low. I still had a mentality where I thought I deserved the abuse. Now I see that I don't deserve it. I deserve happiness just like everybody else. I am glad that Mateo didn't just kill them for hurting me. I'm glad they are getting a second chance. I really think they're done messing with me now.

Kai lets out his breath in a huff. "Mateo isn't the only one who wanted to kill those girls."

I turn to him and notice his eyes are white. There are sparks flying out of his hand, so I put my hand on his cheek trying to get his attention off Brittany and Angela. "They're not worth the effort, Kai. What they did to me sucked, but I am stronger because of what happened. And the rest of

Mateo's pack actually sort of like me because they know I spared them. Good has come from forgiving them."

He turns away from them and looks at me, his eyes changing from white to purple and then light pink. "You're a far better woman than I am as a man."

Before when my mates would say things like that, I always thought it was just to make me feel better. But now that we are bonded I can literally *feel* the truth in his words. Kai knows that I am a good person.

Tears press against the back of my eyes. "Even after knowing everything, I can't believe you still think I'm a good person."

"What we know doesn't change a thing, Layla Rosewood. You're still the kindest, most softhearted person I know. Sometimes, I think you're too nice." He traces his thumb along my cheekbone. "But I suppose that is what makes you, *you*."

I shut my book, looking up at him through my lashes. "You know, I'm done with my homework now."

He grins. "Let's go back to the room. I think Levi would like to watch."

I look around the library, noticing that it is pretty crowded. We probably shouldn't have sex with all these shifters around. Not only would they be able to hear us, but once we were done, they'd be able to smell exactly what we had done in there. Even though we're mated, I still don't want all the other shifters to know.

I stand up from my chair and gather all my books, stuffing them into my bag. Once everything is packed away, he grabs my bag, putting it over his shoulder. I know he doesn't carry my bag because he thinks I'm weak, he does it to be a gentleman. That is something Tucker taught me, and I think it's sweet.

He grabs onto my hand, and my heart feels so full.

I didn't think happiness would be attainable after what Alpha George declared at that trial, but I should've known better. My mates don't care about my parentage. They only care about *me*.

I will never have to be alone again.

Monday, September 19

I put a spell on you.

I wake up with a smile on my face.

Today is going to be a good day. I don't even care that it's Monday and we have five full days until the weekend. I just have a good feeling. And how could I not when I wake up lying between Kai and Levi.

Levi rests his hand right on my boob. I grin, pushing his hand off of me. He complains about me getting up, but I have to shower and get ready for school. I don't bother washing my hair, just because I don't feel like messing with it, and I get dressed as quickly as I can, not wanting to hog the bathroom.

I love sharing a room with my mates, it's incredible, but sharing one bathroom isn't as fun. But our room really wasn't meant for *five* people, it was meant for two—a mated couple. Having four mates is unique, even in the shifter world.

Once I'm ready, Tucker goes into the bathroom to take a quick shower. Mateo, Kai, and Levi took their showers last night. We've had to make a sort of 'shower schedule' with all of us having to share, though the guys say I don't have to follow a schedule. I think they're doing it to be sweet, but I don't want special treatment because I'm the girl.

I flatten my hands over the front of my pleated skirt. We all wear the same uniform. Some of us alter it, but everybody still ends up looking the same.

My skirt initially went down to my knees, but Zoey said I looked like a dork, so she had one of the other girls hem it shorter. It goes to my mid-thigh now, which I admit is a more comfortable length for me. Plus, my mates seem to like this length a lot better too. I notice them all checking out my legs a lot more often now.

Tucker comes out of the bathroom fully dressed. He rubs a towel over his hair, drying it as he walks out. "Ready for breakfast? I'm starved."

I raise an eyebrow. "Don't you want to brush your hair?"

He laughs. "I never brush my hair. Why would I start now?"

Indeed, why?

Boys.

Tucker grabs onto one hand as we head into the hallway and Kai grabs the other. Mateo, as always, walks in the front, and Levi follows behind. I think they like to make a circle around me, trying to protect me. Not that they *have* to protect me from anybody anymore. I'm so glad that Brittany and Angela have moved on from their days of torturing me.

When we walk into the dining hall, the room is shockingly quiet and everybody has their eyes trained on the five of us, or more specifically, me.

"Do I have something on my face?" I lean over, whispering to Kai.

"Ignore them." The annoyance is clear in his voice.

I thought we were over everybody staring at us. I thought they had all grown used to the idea of the five of us being mates.

Well, I guess I do smell like all four guys now that we've all completed the mate bond. But I thought enough people had seen us this weekend that it wouldn't be gossip today.

Tucker's grip on my hand tightens as he and Kai walk us over to our usual table in the corner of the room. Levi and Mateo go to grab food for everybody.

"This is weird, right?" I ask, still keeping my voice low. I don't want everybody in the dining hall to hear what we're saying, and I definitely don't want them to know that their stares are bothering me. Still, I sink down in my seat, trying to make myself appear smaller.

Tucker puts his arm around me, pulling me closer against him. His eyes flash yellow and I know he's close to losing control. He can feel how uncomfortable I am because of everybody's stares. I take a deep breath, trying to calm myself down. I don't want to put my mates on edge like this. Even Kai's eyes flicker between purple and white.

I hear footsteps approaching and look up to see Brittany and Angela approaching the table. They both have *huge* smiles on their faces. My stomach sinks at the sight.

I have a bad feeling about whatever is going on.

Will Brittany and Angela never learn their lesson? Are they so daft that they think they can bully me in front of my mates and in front of the entire school without repercussions? They're on *probation*. It's like they want to be sent to Supernatural Island, or worse. I don't think Mateo would hesitate to kill the two of them. He still wants to, even after the trial.

"Turn around and walk away or this is going to get ugly," Kai threatens as Brittany and Angela come to a stop in front of the table. His entire body is glowing and I can feel the power building inside of him, ready to burst forward.

"It's sickening how you've tricked them into believing they're your mates." Brittany leans down, getting her eyes level with me. "Tell me, what spell did you use? Did you learn it from your bitch—I mean *witch*—mom?"

My heart stops for a moment before it starts galloping. My entire body feels numb and my ears begin to ring as I look at Brittany.

She knows.

"It's disgusting," Angela snarls. "Your mom used a spell to *rape* Alpha George. It's so vile I can hardly stand to look at you."

Rape him?

Why would they think that?

From Alpha George's story, there was no 'raping' involved. He very much liked what he and my birth mother did. I feel sick to my stomach just thinking about it. The only spell she used was for fertility, which is disgusting enough, but that was *her*, not me.

"Enough," Kai yells, thrusting his hands forward. A small burst of power smacks Angela in the face. Her head whips back and her skin turns red where it hit.

Angela covers her cheek with her hand, looking at Kai. "You're not *actually* mated to her. It's a trick. She's a witch. Why do you protect her?"

The dining hall is dead silent as they watch everything unfold at our table. Everybody is curious, but nobody seems surprised.

I guess this explains the stares. Somebody found out the truth about who my biological parents are and they spread the information around to everybody in the school. I just don't know *how* the truth got out. None of the alphas would tell that.

Unless…

Maybe Alpha George told the panthers.

I glance over to where the panthers are sitting, and they are all looking at me with disgust on their faces. They really think that my mom *raped* my dad. They think I'm an abomination.

My eyes leave their table and I look toward where the bears are sitting. They are looking at me with equal disgust.

They believe what Brittany and Angela are saying. They think I cast a spell on my mates to make them mine.

"I'm not even a witch." I look at Brittany and Angela, sitting up straighter. I'm not going to let them smear my name, not now. I have been bullied my whole life. Brittany and Angela are practically amateur. "I'm a panther, or can you not smell over the stench of your own perfume?"

Brittany slaps a hand down on the table. "I'm sure you are able to hide your witchy scent, just like your mom did when she raped Alpha George."

I hear something clatter to the ground. Brittany's body goes rigid at the noise.

I look over and see Mateo racing this way, Levi hot on his trail.

Mateo grabs Brittany by the neck, holding her up so she can't breathe. "What did I fucking tell you about messing with my mate? Do you have a death wish?"

Brittany can't respond because she can't breathe. She claws at his fingers on her neck.

"Mateo." I stand up from the table. "She's not worth it."

But he doesn't listen, he just squeezes her neck tighter.

Panicked, I look at Kai for help and he just shrugs. He doesn't want Mateo to stop. None of my mates want him to stop.

This is what they've wanted since Brittany and Angela attacked me in that bathroom. They want the two of them dead for what they did to me.

"Please, Mateo." I plead with him. "It doesn't matter what they say. You and I know the truth. It will blow over. Just don't kill her. Not here and not now."

Mateo suddenly drops her, but he doesn't do it gently. Brittany falls onto the ground and she kicks her way away from him a few feet.

"Come near my mate again and I will finish what I started." Mateo growls out the words.

"Sorry, Alpha." Angela bows at Mateo, and then reaches a hand out to help her friend off the floor. The two of them scurry off like the rats that they are.

Mateo turns to everybody in the cafeteria and he growls—his voice full-on sounds like a bear. All at once, everybody casts their gaze downward, not looking at us. His body is trembling as his bear is close to the surface.

"I guess I'll get more food," Levi suggests.

Right.

Because ours is currently in a pile on the floor.

I put my head down on the table and groan—it's going to be a long day.

Is it true?

I can barely eat breakfast. My stomach is in knots, but I manage to eat a couple of breakfast burritos, only at Mateo's insistence.

I'm trying not to let what happened get to me. I'm trying to be strong and brave, but it's hard to be after *that.* I realize now that what Alpha George did in the courtroom was just for fun. This was his true plan—to make me *suffer*. He wants to ensure that the abuse I got while in his pride carries on into my new pack too. And he's doing a great job. He's turned them all against me.

This isn't the end, though. It will take a while, but eventually Mateo's pack will see.

I'm not a witch. I'm just a panther. Sure, I only exist because of a spell, but that doesn't change who or what I am. I'm a shifter, just like the rest of them.

As we finish up breakfast, Zoey approaches our breakfast table. She has her lips pursed into a hard line and she's hugging her arms around her middle. She's probably upset about what Brittany and Angela did. I love that I have a friend to look after me like she does. It's sweet.

"Layla, can we talk alone?" Zoey's voice is tight.

I tilt my head to the side. "Yeah."

"No," Mateo growls at his sister. "I will not leave Layla alone. You saw what happened when I was just getting her food."

I roll my eyes. "I had it under control. And I was with Kai and Tucker. They would've stopped it before it went too far."

Mateo turns his hard gaze to me. "They're *my* pack and it's my job to protect you from them."

I flinch at the harshness of his voice and lower my head. "Sorry."

"Mateo, don't be a dick to our mate." I can hear the threat in Tucker's voice.

I glance up at Tucker and see that he has his eyes narrowed at Mateo.

This isn't what I want—for us to be fighting. It's what Alpha George wants. It's why he orchestrated this whole thing.

"I need to talk to Layla without the four of you listening in. It's important." Zoey relaxes her arms at her sides, turning her gaze to her brother. "Please, Mateo."

"Fine, but not here." Mateo sighs, getting up from the table.

The bell rings, alerting us that class is about to start. The dining hall begins to clear out, but it looks like I'm going to be late today. Whatever Zoey needs to say is urgent and I owe it to her to listen. She's been such a good friend to me, and I want to do the same for her.

Mateo leads us out of the dining hall and down a less crowded hallway. He finds an empty classroom and pushes open the door, glancing inside to make sure it's really empty.

"In here," he grumbles.

Zoey walks past me and inside the room first. Her shoulders are tucked tightly into herself as she walks by me, like she's afraid to touch me. It's then that I realize—this conversation is not going to be an easy one.

I go to follow her, but Tucker gently grabs my arm to stop me.

"Are you sure you want to go in there?"

I nod once and he lets go of my arm, but he frowns. I can tell he'd rather me stay with him. My mates want to protect me from this fallout, but they can't. I have to face this head on. I need to set the record straight for Zoey so she doesn't hate me. I need her to *not* believe what the others are saying.

I cast one last glance at my mates before I gently shut the door and turn to face Zoey.

Zoey is standing a few feet away from the door with her arms crossed tightly over her chest. She is looking at me with something I've never seen her direct at me before. Usually these glares are reserved for Brittany and Angela.

"Is it true?" Her voice is strong and harsh.

Chills erupt on my skin, and I realize it's because of her voice. I've never seen her this mad before—not at *anybody*, and it's terrifying.

"What part?" I ask, needing her to clarify.

Her arms drop and she shakes her head. "About your mom. Is she a witch?"

Tears press against the back of my eyes. "Yes."

She silently looks at me, her eyes flashing between black and brown. I've seen her brother do this often, but never because of *me*. It's usually because he's angry with somebody else or on my behalf. It's terrifying to see her so pissed at me.

"Did she really rape your old alpha?" She turns her head, not looking me in the eyes.

"No." I shake my head, denying it. "Alpha George and her had a one night stand, but she didn't force him, at least not according to Alpha George. I've never met the woman who gave birth to me. I guess she used some kind of fertility spell."

Zoey gives me a sharp nod. "So you're half witch?"

I shake my head, then nod. "No, but kind of. My mom is a witch, but I am a full shifter. I didn't get any of her witchy mojo, which is why she dumped me with Alpha George to begin with. I wasn't of any use to her without powers."

She grits her teeth. "How could you do this to my brother?"

I open my mouth to speak, but I'm not sure what to say to her. What does she think I did to her brother? It's not like I can control *who* my parents are, and I definitely can't control the fact that the whole school now knows who my parents are. I'd rather nobody know.

"One guy wasn't enough for you? You had to put your spell on *four* guys who think they're bonded to you." She wrinkles her nose. "It's disgusting. *You* are disgusting. If you have a shred of decency inside of you, you would break the spell and walk away. And if you don't, you'll have me to deal with."

My entire body tenses and my heart races.

Zoey doesn't believe me. She thinks I really 'cast a spell' on her brother. She doesn't think our mate bond is real. Doesn't she know that you can't fake a mate bond? I don't know much about magic, but I do know that there is no spell that could make me feel the way I do about my mates. *Fate* picked them out for me.

"Don't come near me again." She storms past me and out the door. She stomps down the hallway and I stand in the empty classroom, my heart breaking.

I just lost the one and only friend I've ever had.

How could Zoey think that I really cast a spell on her brother? That I cast a spell on all the guys? Does she really think so little of me?

Tears roll down my face as I stand there in complete shock.

She hates me.

What if I'm the villain?

Mateo is pissed at Zoey.

I'm ninety percent certain that if she wasn't his little sister, she wouldn't still be breathing. But I'm *glad* she's his sister. I don't want him to punish everyone who doesn't like me. Everybody is entitled to their own opinion. I just wish I could make her and everybody else in the pack see that I'm *not* the villain they think I am.

But Zoey…

She was my *best friend.* And if she thinks that I did this, that I cast a spell on the guys, then maybe she's right.

I know in my heart that I didn't do it on purpose. I would never. But what if I do have some form of witchcraft and I was just so lonely that it forced this bond upon the guys?

I put up a wall in my mind, not wanting the guys to know what I'm thinking. I know I shouldn't hide it, but if they doubted me, it would kill me. Now that I know what it's like to be bonded and what it's like to mate, I can't go back to the way things were.

Mateo is a good person. But if I tricked him, he would hate me just like Zoey does. There is no way he would want me in his pack anymore. He would send me back to Alpha George, and the abuse would start all over again.

I pull my knees up to my chest, hugging them.

The guys decided that we're skipping school the rest of the day. I know that I should object—we've already skipped enough school—but the thought of going today and having everybody stare at me, for them to judge me, it's too much.

Kai puts his hand on my leg. "You know, just because you block your thoughts from us doesn't mean we can't feel your emotions. I can feel the self-loathing coming off of you right now. I hate it, Layla."

"Sorry." I didn't mean to make this harder on my mates. I want to protect them in all of this, just as much as they want to protect me.

"You need to calm down."

I look over at Tucker, wondering why he's telling me to calm down, but I see that he's got a hand on Mateo's shoulder.

Mateo is visibly shaking. He's filled with rage, and I know it's because he feels responsible. He thinks his pack is the reason I feel bad. It's not just Brittany and Angela, but Zoey too. He's so mad that he's having problems controlling his bear.

"Maybe we should go for a run," Levi suggests.

Kai nods. "Yeah. I'll stay here with Layla. You guys should go."

Mateo's black eyes meet mine, his shoulders tight. I can tell he's about to tell them no, but he needs this desperately. He needs to relieve the tension and anger that is building before it explodes.

"Go," I tell him softly. "I promise I'll be fine. Kai is here with me."

Without a word, Mateo turns and walks to the door. He throws it open with such force I'm surprised it didn't rip right off its hinges. But then again, this castle has been remodeled from the days when fairies owned it. We've reinforced everything because shifters have tempers, especially alphas.

Levi follows Mateo out the door, and Tucker immediately behind Levi. He waves at me as he shuts the door behind them. I have a feeling they're going to be gone for a little while. Mateo has a lot of steam he needs to let loose.

I'm thankful that they're gone. Kai is here, but he sits beside me silently, letting me think. I need to feel what I need to feel, and he won't judge me for that. He will just sit here beside me and hold my hand and tell me everything is going to be all right. That is what I need right now. What I *don't* need is an alpha threatening to kill his entire pack to protect me.

"What if I did force the bond?" Now that the rest of the guys are gone, I'm not as afraid to admit it out loud.

Kai isn't a shifter, so he doesn't know how much shifters despise witches. Well… it's not just a shifter thing. I suppose a lot of supernaturals hate witches. But fairies don't. If anything, the fae can understand witches.

The fae haven't always been liked by other supernaturals. Not because the fae did anything wrong, but because the other supernaturals thought they were too powerful. The supernatural community thought the fae were extinct until about two years ago when the truth came out.

"What are you talking about? You're not even a witch. How could you force the bond?" Kai shakes his head at me, and he doesn't try to block his thoughts from me. He thinks I'm being absurd. "And even if you were a witch, you couldn't force a mate bond. It's impossible."

He doesn't get it.

I guess I shouldn't have expected him to.

"No, you're right." I lower my head, clearing my throat. "Do you want to watch a movie or something?"

He furrows his brows. "Layla, come on. Talk to me."

I shake my head. "I can't, okay? I just need to work it out in my head right now."

"I'm your mate. You should be able to talk to me."

But is he my mate?

My chest aches just thinking it.

I don't want to imagine a world without my guys. Since I met them, everything has come together. It's like my life now has meaning and a purpose. I'm not just the prides' punching bag. And I can't imagine my life and my world without them. They are my everything.

But what if it was all a lie?

What if I did it, even if unintentionally.

The thought of taking something special away from them kills me. What if the magic I used somehow made it so they'll never find their true mate?

Kai rubs at his chest. "Layla, you're killing me here."

"Sorry." I chew on the side of my lip, wishing I could just stop hurting everybody that I love.

"Zoey was out of line in what she said." Kai grabs my hand, looking me right in the eyes. "If she wasn't Mateo's little sister, I would've ended her."

"I'm glad you didn't." Zoey shouldn't be killed for thinking what she did. I can't even blame her for thinking it.

The truth is, I think she's right. The more I think about it, the more sense it makes. My mind tried to reject it at first. You can't fake a mate bond. But maybe they're all wrong. And maybe Kai is stuck with me because I forced him into it, even if it was unintentional.

Kai leans forward, kissing me on the forehead. I savor the way his lips feel on my skin.

It's selfish of me to think that even if I did somehow force our bond, I still wouldn't take anything back. I love Kai. I love *all* of them. And I'm tired of being alone.

"What if I'm the villain?" I ask Kai, needing to say the words out loud.

He grins, pulling me closer to him. "Then you're the nicest villain I've ever seen. And I'll gladly be your slave for all eternity."

I laugh, but his words strike a thought within me.

I don't want to force these guys to be with me.

All this time I felt bad for my mates for being stuck with a runt like me. Now I know that it's worse than I even imagined it could be.

"I love you, Layla."

My breath catches in my throat and tears press against the back of my eyes. "I love you too."

But are his feelings true?

I don't know if I'll ever find the answer.

I fucking love you.

When Levi, Mateo, and Tucker get back later, I'm still coping. Or, as Kai is thinking, I'm *moping*. But he would be moping too if he would only realize what I did to him—what I did to all of them. I forced this bond on him, and I forced them to love me. That's not okay.

Levi huffs, sitting down on the mattress in front of me. I was mindlessly watching a random superhero movie Kai put on, but I wasn't really paying attention.

"Hey, I'm watching that." I pout.

I'm not really watching it carefully. I'm more like staring at the screen, thinking about how awful of a person I am.

"No, you weren't," Levi says, stubbornly refusing to get out of my way.

I scoot over so I can see around him.

Levi gets up, grabbing the remote off the nightstand, and makes a big show of pointing the remote at the screen and shutting it off.

"You know you don't have to point the remote. It does have a sensor." I only say it because I feel like being a smart-ass. Levi can really invoke an overly emotional response from me.

He sits back on the bed, getting right in my face. "I don't care about the stupid remote. I just want your attention."

I cross my arms over my chest. "Well, you *have* my attention. So say whatever you need to say."

Tucker, Kai, and Mateo all stand wordlessly behind Levi as he gets in my face. Usually they'd have stopped him, but now, I get the feeling Levi is doing what they all wish they could right now. They aren't going to stop him.

"You think you're good at blocking us, but you're not." Levi's voice is harsher than I've ever heard it before. "You think you somehow magically *forced* this mate bond on us."

I swallow hard.

This is it.

He's going to tell me he knows it's magically forced. Now that it's been pointed out, he hates me.

He shakes his head. "You're wrong. That's not what I'm going to say."

"It's not?" I look at him, my eyes wide.

"No. You know what I'm going to say?" He takes a breath, leaning close. "I don't *care* if you forced this mate bond on me. You didn't, just to be clear, but even if you did, it doesn't change how I feel about you. You are more than just my mate. You're my everything, Layla."

His words take my breath away.

I rub a hand at the base of my throat. "How can you say that, Levi? I forced this mate bond on you."

"No. You didn't." He groans. "You can't fake a mate bond. It's not possible. And if you weren't being so stubborn right now, you would realize it too. Even if you had been studying magic your whole life, the spell simply doesn't exist. If it did, don't you think some witch would've exploited it by now?"

"I… guess…" I rub at my chin, considering his words.

"It's simply not possible. But if it were, there is no way that an untrained witch could accidentally force the bond. It just wouldn't happen."

I open my mouth to protest, because certainly he's wrong. There has to be a flaw in his thinking. But the more I consider his words, the more I realize they're true.

I have spent all this time blindly believing that I forced this on the guys. I didn't even take the time to consider that it didn't even make sense. I guess I just believed Zoey because she's my friend. I would never think that she would lie to me.

"When Zoey accused me…" A tear rolls down my cheek, and my thoughts cut off.

I don't want Mateo to be mad at his sister. I still love her, even though she thinks the worst about me. I have to believe she will come around. She's my friend.

"Are you sure?" I look up at Levi through my lashes.

"I fucking love you. Please never doubt that, and never doubt the bond that we share." He gently wipes at the tears on my cheeks.

"I fucking love you too." I don't normally cuss, but if he's going to say it, so am I.

The guys all laugh, and some of the tension leaves my body.

"I don't think I've ever heard you cuss." Levi grins, shaking his head. "It was kind of hot."

"She said the f-word before." Tucker comes forward, his eyes on me. "When we completed our mate bond for the first time, she begged me to fuck her."

My face grows warm.

Yeah, that did happen.

"It's not fair to hold anything I said against me when we're mating." Because I was turned on, and clearly not thinking straight. The only thing I knew was that I wanted Tucker. I won't apologize for that.

It's suddenly very hot in here.

"No more dark thoughts, right?" Levi asks, scooting closer to me.

"I'll try." It's not something I can promise, but it is something I am working on. I've been working on it since I met the guys. It's not easy to go from thinking you're weak, ugly, and disgusting then have a complete one-eighty practically overnight. I can feel myself getting better. I know my worth now. My guys have taught me my worth.

I'm not garbage like Alpha George thinks. And my mother who threw me away? Who cares what she thinks. She didn't even want me in her life. So be it. I have four incredible men who love me unconditionally. It's not because of the mate bond either. They just love me, period.

For Levi to say it wouldn't matter if there was a bond or not… that means everything to me.

"We all feel that way." Kai steps forward. His eyes are somewhere between gray and purple, which makes me feel guilty.

When Kai's eyes are gray, that means he's sad. I hurt him. I hurt all of them. I can't believe I did that.

Why do I have to always be so stubborn?

"It's not your fault." Mateo sits down on the edge of the mattress, close to me. "You didn't start thinking that until after what my sister said. She was the one who was wrong. She was out of line. I will be having a talk with her tomorrow."

"No," I protest, shaking my head. "I want Zoey to make up her own mind about me. I don't want her to be forced into talking to me because her big brother and future alpha forced her to. I need her to come to me herself. And I do think she will come, eventually. She just has to learn how to trust me again."

I don't blame her for thinking the things she does about me. I would probably think them too in her shoes. She's just being a good little sister and looking out for her older brother.

"I don't like it. I need to protect you from everybody, even my little sister." His voice breaks, and it's then that I see how much this has bothered him. He is just as upset by what Zoey said as I am.

I reach a hand out and touch his arm. "Just try to forget about it, okay? I will never ask you to choose between Zoey and me. Even if she hates me, she's your sister. She's important."

He nods, but he doesn't relax.

I know he wants things to work out between Zoey and me. I do too. But that's on her.

"Let's just put all the craziness behind us for now," I suggest. "We can see if the kitchen will make us fifty pizzas and we can have a movie day."

Levi snorts. "Fifty pizzas? Even we can't eat that many."

I don't know about that. They can eat a lot.

"A movie night sounds awesome." Kai flops onto the bed right beside me. "But please don't let Levi pick the movie. If

I have to watch another Sci-Fi movie, I'm going to vomit. Everybody knows aliens aren't real."

Kai's statement causes everybody to debate the existence of aliens. And maybe it's a completely mundane and weird thing to even talk about considering everything that has happened, but it's exactly what I need. I need these moments of normalcy with the guys.

I know now that the five of us will be able to make it through literally anything that life decides to throw our way. Things have been difficult, but there is finally a rainbow after the storm.

I'm so happy, I feel like my heart could burst.

I was so wrong.

Later that night after we're finished eating way too much pizza, there is a knock on the door. I have no idea who would be coming over to see us, but I am anxious. Usually when somebody comes to our door, it's Alpha Scott saying that he needs Mateo. I just don't want Mateo to leave tonight. I want all of my mates here because they've made my day so much better.

"I'm not going anywhere." Mateo kisses me on the top of the head before getting out of bed.

I know he says that, but he can't say no to his alpha. I wouldn't want him to either. We should respect our alpha's wishes, even if it's not what we want.

Mateo's entire body tenses up as he opens the door. I don't see who is on the other side because he slams the door shut.

There is another knock, this time more insistent.

"Open up," a familiar voice yells from the other side. "Please, Mateo."

I know that voice.

I sit up as I realize that Zoey is on the other side of the door.

"Mateo." My voice barely comes out above a whisper and my heart is beating so fast. "Please don't shut your sister out because of me. It would kill me to think that I ruined your relationship. I know how important she is to you."

He shakes his head. "No. If she can't accept you, she can't be in my life."

"At least hear her out," I urge, knowing that he will regret it if he doesn't at least try. I can't be the reason Mateo and his sister get into a feud. I refuse to pull his family apart, especially after how welcoming and kind they've been to me. Zoey and I will work out our differences in time, I know that. "There has been enough fighting already, don't you think?"

He grunts and I can tell he's close to giving in.

"Please, Mateo." Zoey's voice breaks as she yells from the other side, and I don't have to see her to know that she's crying.

Mateo hesitantly opens the door. "Why should I let you in after how you talked to my mate?"

I want to tell him not to be so hard on her, but Mateo needs this. He needs to know why his sister hurt me the way she did. And it's then that I realize, Zoey didn't just hurt me. She hurt Mateo deeply. So I keep my mouth shut and I let Mateo have this moment with his little sister.

"I know. I screwed up, okay?" She sniffs.

"You did." Mateo crosses his arms over his chest. "Today, you showed Layla that you're not any better than her old pride. You acted like… Brittany and Angela, but instead of using your fists, you used words. And Layla didn't do anything to deserve the way you treated her. She's been nothing but kind to you. Why would you do that?"

"I don't know, okay?" She sobs. "I just heard those rumors and I thought—"

"You thought what?" Mateo cuts her off. "That the girl who convinced me not to kill Brittany and Angela after they beat the hell out of her is actually a bad person? You think that my mate, who has the biggest heart of anybody I've ever known, is capable of the monstrous things that you accused her of?"

Zoey doesn't say anything back. I imagine she's standing there in stunned silence, but I can't see around Mateo to her.

"Even if Layla was a witch, I wouldn't care. It doesn't change how I feel about her." Mateo lets out his breath in a huff. "Just, use your nose, Zoey. I know that witches are capable of hiding their scent, but they can only do it for a short period of time. She's been here for a month now. And I'm *in her head.* We've completed our mate bond and she is mine. Don't you think I'd know if she was hiding something? She's not. Well, that's not exactly true. She is hiding something. But only the abuse she received at her old pride. She's worried I'm going to murder all the panthers, because she's a fucking angel."

"I'm sorry."

"It's not me you should say sorry to," Mateo says. "And if she decides to not forgive you, I will stand beside her. I love you, Zoey, and I always will, but my mate comes first now. She's my everything."

My mouth falls open as I process Mateo's words to his sister.

I don't want to put a wedge between them, but hearing him say those words to his sister warms my heart in a strange way.

I wasn't doubting Mateo's love for me. I *know* he loves me. I can feel it with every fiber of my being. But hearing him say those words out loud, and feeling the truth behind them, touches me in a way that I can't describe.

Zoey will always be part of our lives. I hope that she will be an important part. Not just as my sister-in-law, to put it in human terms, but also as my friend and confidant. I have a feeling I'm going to need a girl friend considering I have four mates. I love them, but sometimes I just need to have girl time. The thought of losing Zoey makes my chest ache.

"Can I come in?" Zoey asks Mateo. I can hear the hope in her voice.

Mateo sighs, stepping back. "Fine. But we are not leaving you alone with Layla. Not now and maybe not ever again, not until I trust that you won't hurt her."

"That is fair." Zoey takes a step forward and into our room. I don't see her until Mateo moves to shut the door once she's entered.

Zoey looks rough. Her face is red, like she's spent a lot of time crying, and her hair is messy. Zoey normally looks perfect. Even when we're training and I'm a sweaty mess, her hair is always perfect—never a strand out of place. And I've definitely never seen her without makeup before. She doesn't need it, her skin is flawless, but today she looks like she's been to hell and back.

A tear escapes, trailing down her face when she sees me. "I'm sorry."

Those words bring tears to my own eyes because I wasn't expecting her to apologize. And if she did apologize, I thought she would just do it for Mateo's sake. But when she looks at me, I can see that her apology has nothing to do with Mateo and everything to do with me.

"I heard what everybody was saying about you and I believed them." She shakes her head, running her fingers through her hair. "I feel so stupid, because I know how Brittany and Angela are. I tried to fight the rumor at first, but when everybody kept saying it, I realized it might not be a rumor. So I approached you. I hoped you would tell me it was a lie. But when you said it was true, I snapped. I thought that you cast a spell on my brother, but I was wrong. I knew almost immediately after I left that classroom that I screwed up. I didn't know what to do though. I called my mom and she told me what happened during that trial. She told me all the awful things Alpha George said about you. She told me to apologize to you and make things right. But apologizing just doesn't feel like enough. I screwed up, Layla. And I don't expect you or my brother to ever forgive me. Family should never treat each other the way I treated you."

At the end of her speech, there are tears rolling down both of our faces. I am a sobbing mess as I get off the bed and walk over to her. I throw my arms around her, squeezing her tight. She holds me just as tightly against her, and we cry together.

I realize in that moment, Zoey isn't just a friend. She's my sister, my family. Sometimes families fight. And forgiving her is the easiest thing I have ever done.

"I forgive you." I whisper the words to her, knowing she can hear me.

Her entire body relaxes into mine and she squeezes me even tighter against her.

"You're my sister and I love you," I tell her as we pull back. "But don't ever do that again or I'll punch you."

She laughs through her tears. "When did you become a badass?"

"My alpha is training me." I shrug, like it's not a big deal.

"If I ever talk to you like that again, you have permission to punch me." She folds her hands in front of her. "I'm serious."

I think I might. I mean, better me punch her than Mateo.

"And I love you too. I also consider you my sister." She smiles widely.

I have a sister.

Tuesday, September 20

What a horrible way to die.

I am incredibly happy today. Nothing can bring me down—not the stares from other shifters, not the whispers, and definitely not the rumors about me.

So what if I'm half witch? My mates accept me for who I am. And, more importantly, *I* accept me for who I am.

When I met my mates, I only cared about getting their approval and their love. Those things are still important to me. But I've also learned that I need to love myself. If I can't love myself, then how can anybody else love me?

It's a liberating feeling when you stop caring about what others think. I know it'll take me a little while to adjust to the change, but I'm working on it for me. And to do something like this for myself feels incredible.

After Supernatural History, Kai walks me to my next class, Modern English. I have my next class with Tucker and I'm eager to see him. I always get anxious when I'm away from my mates for any extended period of time. I know that it's just because our bond is so new, but I don't mind anyway. I like being with my mates.

"I need to go to the bathroom," I tell Kai, as I come to a stop outside of one of the bathrooms on the main floor.

He frowns. "We can go back to the room."

"We don't have time, and I think we've both skipped enough classes." I smirk, shaking my head. "It'll take me two minutes to pee. I'll be quick."

"Fine." He leans against the wall outside of the bathroom. "But I will be waiting right here for you."

I laugh at his protectiveness. It's cute, even if it's not necessary. "I love you. Be right back."

"Love you too." He grins, revealing dimples.

Gah, he's incredible.

I open the bathroom and walk inside. A couple of girls are in the stall, but after a quick sniff I realize that they smell like bears, so I'm not worried. If they were panthers, I would turn around and walk out of the bathroom, especially after what happened with Alpha George the other day. I have a feeling he still has a few tricks up his sleeve. He's not going to make leaving the pride easy.

After finishing going to the bathroom, I go to wash my hands, scrubbing extra hard. I probably should have gone back to the room. Public bathrooms are always gross, even in our school where they try their best to keep them clean. Teenage girls are nasty, no matter what their species.

"Well, well… look who we have here. A runt all on her own."

I flinch at the sound of Brittany's voice, but I try to ignore her as I wash the soap from my hands. I turn off the water, shaking water from my hands. I don't even bother grabbing a paper towel. I'll just leave my hands wet so I don't have to deal with Brittany. But before I can reach the bathroom door, Angela steps in front of it, flicking the lock shut.

"We've been wanting to get you alone again for a long time now. It's hard when you've always got a bodyguard. But you're alone now," Brittany taunts.

"Kai is waiting outside," I warn them.

I am careful to keep my thoughts blocked from him, not wanting him to knock down the door and rescue me. There has been enough gossip in the school about me as it is.

Angela snorts. "The fae? He's a runt like you."

I roll my eyes. "Kai isn't a runt, and neither am I, you bitch."

"Wow." Brittany looks at Angela, a smirk on her face. "The kitty has claws."

"Is that supposed to be funny?" It's ironic that she's calling me a 'kitty.' I'm a panther—a predator.

"You came to school here, stole our alpha and our pack, but we're not going to let you get away with it. Not anymore." Angela and Brittany both advance on me.

But I've been training. Maybe not as much as I'd like, but what time Mateo spends training me I learn a lot. When Angela swings her first punch at me, I block it. She stumbles backward in shock.

How's that for a runt?

Brittany swings her arm at me and I move out of the way. Her fist meets air.

"That's it," Brittany grunts.

She and Angela advance on me, kicking and punching. And while I have learned a lot about fighting and blocking, there are still two of them and one of me. It's not really a fair fight. I hear a pounding on the door and I know Kai is about to break into the bathroom. I can fight them off until he gets in here.

But something reflective catches my eye and I look down to see Brittany swinging a silver knife at my chest. I move out of the way just in time, but she swings again, hitting me in the stomach this time. I scream as the silver blade cuts into my skin.

This is it. These two bullies are really going to kill me this time.

I put a hand to my wound, trying to stop the bleeding as Brittany makes another swing. This time the blade slashes across my arm.

Unable to fight any longer, I fall to my knees. Brittany lifts up the blade, ready to shove the thing into my chest. I close my eyes and say my goodbyes to my mates, but the last stab never comes. Or maybe it does, I don't know, because suddenly everything gets quiet and the world around me gets hazy.

I see big blurs of people rushing in as I lie down on the floor—well, more like fall onto the floor. My head hits the concrete, making a sickening thud. I'm aware of the warm, thick puddle that surrounds me, and then there is nothing. Just darkness.

What should we do with them?

I come to with my head on something soft and warm.

"Layla, wake up, baby." Somebody is shaking me. I'm not ready to open my eyes yet, but their voice is so frantic.

When my eyes open, I immediately shut them again, squeezing them tight. The light is blindingly bright and my ears are ringing.

"Layla." I feel a presence around me, so I finally open my eyes.

I'm lying on the bathroom floor in a puddle of my own blood. Tucker is holding something to the wound on my stomach to stop the blood from flowing, but the cut isn't as bad as I first thought it was. It's not even that deep. And the cut on my arm barely even stings.

I look up and see that I am lying in Kai's lap. He gently strokes my hair. Levi is kneeling beside Tucker, his eyes wide as he looks at me.

Still, I glance around a little more, trying to find Mateo. He is standing on the other side of the room with his back turned toward me. He turns around, as if he senses me looking at him, and that's when I realize what he was doing. Brittany and Angela are both tied up on the other side of the room, their eyes wide with panic.

Good.

As bad as it sounds, I *want* them to feel fear right now. After everything they've put me through, they deserve to feel an ounce of the fear that they've caused me.

"What should we do with them?" Mateo growls out the words, as his bear is close to the surface.

I'm shocked that he's asking me. His bear is *demanding* that he end them. He's shaking from holding back. But I know that he's holding back for me.

Part of me wants to forgive them and let them go. But I tried that once, hoping that it would be enough. It wasn't. Brittany and Angela can never seem to stop coming after me. This time, they almost killed me, and they would have if my mates hadn't stopped them. If I forgive them, I would live in constant fear. I'd always have to have a bodyguard with me everywhere, even in the bathroom, and that is no way to live.

I look at Tucker. He is shaking in anger as well, but he's trying to stay focused on me. He's wanting Mateo to kill the two girls so we can end this and he can take me to see the doctor.

Kai's eyes are glowing and while he's trying to be okay with whatever I choose for Brittany and Angela, he knows that the only thing he'll be happy with is death. He thinks it's what they deserve.

I turn my focus to Levi. He's gently stroking my hand, but he is restraining himself. He wants to *end* them. He thinks that if I decide to forgive them he will still kill them and make it look like an accident. He's contemplating all the ways he can do it without getting caught.

It's then that I know what I have to do.

It's not enough for Brittany and Angela to be banned from the school or the pack. They will never stop coming after me. They've decided to hate me for whatever reasons they think are legit. And if they are alive, it will never end.

I look at Brittany, who is watching me with wide eyes, but even I can see the slight smirk on her face. She thinks I'm going to forgive them again. And Angela glares at me, even at the risk of death.

Turning my attention to Mateo, I frown. "End them."

I don't take any joy in ending their life, but it is the way it has to be.

Mateo nods. "Get her out of here. I'll meet you guys in the doctor's office."

Kai lifts me off the ground into his arms and he carries me from the bathroom. As we're walking out, I hear Brittany start to beg Mateo. I close my eyes, wishing the sounds of her cries to go away. Unlike her, I don't take joy in her death. The death of any shifter is a great loss, and they will both be missed in the pack.

Kai snorts. "I won't miss them."

I grin, but my heart is still heavy. I wonder if I made the right decision.

Kai brings me to the doctor's office. The doctor is waiting for us there, so I think Tucker or Levi must've called and told him that we were on our way.

The doctor gets to work on me, getting my mind off of Brittany and Angela. My arm is fine, he just bandages it up and says it should be healed in two days. But the cut on my stomach is slightly more severe. He has to stitch me up, but he said that the wound should heal within a week or less. It's not nearly as bad as I thought it would be.

As he is finishing up, Levi, Mateo, and Tucker walk in.

I tense up when I see them.

"Is it done?" Kai asks.

Mateo gives a tight nod.

My chest aches a little at the thought.

Brittany and Angela are dead because of me. I could've given them mercy again, but I didn't. I might as well have been the one to end their life.

"I am so proud of you." Tucker walks closer to the bed, squeezing my hand. "You did what was right, and I never want you to doubt that."

Did I though?

"It was the only way they were going to stop," Mateo says. "You were right. If we got them kicked out of school and the pack, they wouldn't have stopped. They blamed you for ruining their life for some reason, and they were obsessed with trying to kill you. It had to be this way."

"Either way, I was going to kill them," Levi admits.

I grin, because I did know that from his thoughts. But who knows if he would've followed through.

"All done," the doctor says.

"Thanks," I tell him.

"The girls who did this to you were bad news. Going after another shifter with silver isn't right. Don't feel guilty for letting your mates protect you." The doctor pushes up from his chair. "And don't let me see you in here again. No more fights."

I laugh. "I'll try."

He offers me a smile as he turns and leaves the room. I go to push myself up, but my stomach is sore so Kai has to help me. Before my feet can even hit the ground, Levi swoops me carefully into his arms, carrying me.

He knows I can walk, so there is no point in even saying it out loud. Plus, I kind of like being held right now. What happened today weighs so heavily on my heart.

"What are you going to tell the pack?" I ask Mateo, as we all walk from the doctor's office toward our room upstairs.

It looks like yet another day I won't be going to school. Probably not tomorrow either because my mates will want me to stay in bed and recover more. Though, now that I'm mated to them, staying in bed all day does kind of sound fun.

"I will tell the pack exactly what happened—that Brittany and Angela cornered you and came at you with a silver knife intending to kill you. They wouldn't stop, so I had to end their lives. I will let them know that nothing comes before protecting your mate, not even your pack." Mateo's response surprises me.

I guess I'm still used to Alpha George. For him, the only thing that was more important than the pride was himself.

Mateo is going to make a great alpha one day. I am proud to be a member of his pack.

Kai opens the door, allowing Levi to carry me through first. He gently lays me down on the bed, kissing my forehead. My mates coddle me, and I am okay with it, because I know they need it just as much as I do.

Love is all consuming and powerful. It's then that I *know* with everything inside of me that this bond wasn't created by magic. Nothing but fate could make me feel like this. And this is just the beginning of our forever.

Parental rights.

Later that evening, I'm feeling a lot better. Better enough that I want to eat dinner in the dining hall. The guys object, but I'm going a little stir crazy, so I talk them into it.

Truthfully, I want to see Zoey. I haven't seen her since she came to apologize last night, and I want to talk to her. I want to make sure things are good between us and not awkward. Though, I guess some awkwardness is to be expected after everything that happened.

I also want to see how the rest of the pack is going to act. Mateo held a pack meeting earlier and told them what happened. He said that it went well and that most people weren't even shocked by the news, but I know that he sometimes likes to say what he thinks I want to hear and what will make me feel better.

Tucker helps me get dressed that evening, and he definitely checks me out while he's doing it. His face turns red as he realizes I've caught him, but I don't have anything to hide from my mates. Not anymore. I'm done trying to block them from my thoughts. From now on, everything is an open book. And my body is his anyway.

"When you're better," he declares, but there is heat in his eyes as he looks at me.

My heart flutters. "I can't wait."

I hope I'm better enough tonight, but I doubt my mates will think so. They'll want to make sure I'm healed up good before we mate again, which makes me sad. I hate waiting.

"That pout," Kai whines. "Why are you so freaking cute, Layla?"

I just grin and shrug. "I'd say it's in my DNA, but we both know who my father is. I must get it from my mom."

Mateo chuckles. "If your mom is as hot as Alpha George described her, I'd say you probably do look like your mom."

I laugh, feeling free about the subject. I can finally joke about who my biological parents are. I've changed so much from the girl who came here. She was timid and scared of everything. Now, I'm getting brave and I'm not scared to speak my mind. I like the woman I'm becoming.

The five of us go to the dining hall together to grab dinner. The guys insist on me sitting down and them delivering the food, which isn't different than how they normally act anyway. So I sit down at the table between Mateo and Tucker while Levi and Kai go to grab food for us all.

When I get in there, everybody does look at me, but only for a moment. I realize that people are done staring. I guess they found something new to talk about, which is a relief. I'm sick of being at the center of school gossip, especially when there are rumors about me being a witch. That was annoying.

Mateo gently bumps his shoulder with mine. "I told you everything was good."

He did.

I guess he wasn't just saying it to make me feel better.

Kai and Levi come back to the table with a couple of platters that are overflowing with food. I'm not even surprised by the amount anymore. I know that my mates will clear their plates too. They can eat so much. Though to be fair, I can eat quite a bit myself these days. Since my body is using a lot of energy to heal itself, I am starving tonight.

Just as I'm about to take a bite of my food, I hear a gasp in the cafeteria. Wondering what everybody is going on about now, I turn to see Alpha Scott, Alpha Mutatio, and Alpha George enter the dining hall together.

This can't be good.

"Layla, we need you to come with us," Alpha Scott declares.

I look at Mateo before standing up. All four of my mates stand up with me, following Alpha Scott and the other alphas from the dining hall. It's not Alpha Scott or the wolf alpha that has me concerned. It's the fact that Alpha George is here. Whenever he's around, it means trouble. So this isn't going to be good.

We follow the alphas into a private room a few doors down from the dining hall and Alpha Scott motions for us to take a seat.

"Alpha George, you have the floor." Alpha Scott's voice is tight and his face is red.

My stomach is in knots while I wait to hear what my old alpha has to say.

"Layla, I will admit that I haven't always been the greatest father to you." Alpha George looks at me, a frown on his face. "I regret it."

"Not the greatest father? Are you mental? You haven't been a father period. The only thing you did is donate your sperm." I wrinkle my nose in disgust as I look at him. "So don't even try to play that card."

Alpha George clears his throat and continues talking as if I never said anything. "I want a second chance, therefore I have decided to invoke my parental rights. It is my right as an alpha to have my daughter be a member of my pride. It's where you belong."

I shake my head. "I am not going back to your pride."

"I'm afraid you don't have a choice." Alpha Scott pales as he looks at me. "I'm sorry, Layla, but it's the law. Alpha George has rights over you because you're his daughter. There isn't anything I can do."

What the—

The end.

The Forever Girl (Book 3) is coming soon!

Letter from Scarlett.

I can't believe I just typed 'the end' on this book.

The Lost Girl was therapeutic for me. I had a blast writing it, and I hope you love it too. It was fun to try new plotting techniques.

Layla really grows a lot in this story. I wanted to give her a reason to be strong. And I knew by putting her through what I did, she would come out stronger on the other side. I'm happy with the development and I'm really excited to write the next book and see where the story takes me.

If you did enjoy this book, it would mean a lot to me if you left a review wherever you picked this up.

For more information on this series, be sure to check out my blog https://scarletthaven.net!

Also, if you really like my books, join my Facebook group, The Haven. We just like to hang out, and have fun. Sometimes I give away advanced copies of my books, and sneak peeks of upcoming releases. https://www.facebook.com/groups/1899968653639439

—**Scarlett Haven**

More books by Scarlett

Elite Academy:
Mystic Academy (Prequel)
Vampire School (Book 1)
Vampire Born (Book 2—coming soon!)

Shifter Academy: United:
The New Girl (Book 1)
The Lost Girl (Book 2)
The Forever Girl (Book 3—coming soon!)

Spy Academy:
The Undercover Life (Book 1)
My Dirty Secrets (Book 2)
If I Go Rogue (Book 3)
The Secret Intelligence (Book 4)
I'll Never Forget You (Book 5)
*This series is completed.

Tiger Shifter Chronicles:
Concealed (Book 1)
Exposed (Book 2)
Unleashed (Book 3)
*This series is completed.

Dragon Shifter Academy Series:
Dragon Royalty (Book 1)
Dragon Elite (Book 2)
Dragon Guards (Book 3)
Dragon Choice (Book 4)
Dragon Hearts (Book 5)
Dragon Forever (Book 6)
*This series is completed.

The Zara Chronicles:
Loyal (Book 1)
Truth (Book 2)
Toxic (Book 3)
Trust (Book 4)
Chaos (Book 5)
Dream (Book 6)
Jaded (Book 7)
Blame (Book 8)
Power (Book 9)
Vague (Book 10)
Crazy (Book 11)
Adore (Book 12)
*This series is completed.

Shifter Academy Series:
Different (Book 1)
Monster (Book 2)
Hybrid (Book 3)
*This series is completed.

After Spy Series:
Hacked (Book 1)
*This is a stand alone series.

East Raven Academy Series:
Ever After (Book 1)
Never Ever (Book 2)
Never Say Never (Book 3)
For Ever (Book 4)
*This series is completed.

The Spy Chronicles:
Finding Me (Book 1)
Keeping Me (Book 2)
Losing Me (Book 3)

Saving Me (Book 4)
*This series is completed.

Stand alone books:
The Bucket List: Famous Online
The Day My Life Began

Bayside Academy Series:
Gracie (Book 1)
Unraveling Gracie (Book 2)
Hating Gracie (Book 3)
*This series is completed.

Find me online.

Website: https://scarletthaven.net
Twitter: https://twitter.com/Scarlett_Haven
Facebook:
https://www.facebook.com/AuthorScarlettHaven/
Facebook Group:
https://www.facebook.com/groups/1899968653639439
Instagram:
https://www.instagram.com/authorscarletthaven/
Mailing List: https://wordpress.us13.list-manage.com/subscribe?u=2b073ef1d3dd1a8003e58a389&id=8393d2923e

Printed in Poland
by Amazon Fulfillment
Poland Sp. z o.o., Wrocław